RO

RINGS

& SYLVIA

SINGS

AN EROTIC COMEDY OF ERRORS

CHAPTER ONE

Rings and things

Reader…I married him.

I fucking did, I really did! I'm now officially Mrs Dr Gorgeous!   Who would have thought it…Me, Ann without an 'e' a doctor's wife…I've gone from failed erotic goddess to pillar of the community.   I was officially going to be Mrs Ann Monroe…I always knew me and Marilyn had lots in common. Given my dating history, I really had convinced myself that I would end up a crazy cat lady with an extensive collection of dildos. Archie and I had been dating for just over a year and everyday was better than the last.   Everything was utterly perfect and my muff was in a permanent state of bliss…my fanny didn't just tingle it had volcanic tremors. Archie certainly knew how to press all my buttons and over the past year he had pressed them in every way imaginable.

Then, just when I thought it couldn't get any better, he took me for a long weekend in New York and proposed to me at the top of The Empire State Building. It came completely out of the blue and I really wasn't expecting it. When he got down on one knee I wondered what the fuck was going on. I honestly thought he was joking and waited for the punchline. It was only when I heard people starting to clap that I realised. I did try to play it cool…honestly! I tried so hard to be sedate and gracious but excitement got the better of me and attempted to snatch the ring out of his hands, like it was 'my precious'. I watched in absolute horror as my grab for the ultimate prize went spectacularly wrong and I knocked the box out of Archie's grasp. Time ground to a standstill as I watched the beautiful leather box bounce off his shoe causing the ring to depart it's cushioned surround and make a break for freedom…fuck me, this whole thing could be cursed if the ring doesn't want to go on my finger. There was no way I was losing the fucking thing before I'd even had the chance to brag about my engagement! Knocking over chairs and tables as I went, I threw my whole body onto it to stop it bouncing into oblivion. I fished the ring out from between my ample thighs and held it up in the air like the hard earned trophy it was. Disaster averted, I started to ugly cry with joy…I accepted Archie's proposal through happy tears and snot bubbles. The ring was beautiful and it was set with an obscenely large diamond. Seriously that fucker would be my pension if Archie ever left me. We decided not to tell anyone until we returned home. This was our moment and we wanted to savour every second which was really romantic, but I cannot tell you how desperate I was to post it on Facebook…I was literally sitting on my hands until we got back.

Once we were home, the wedding planning began with a vengeance. My Mum was beside herself…her daughter was marrying a doctor which obviously warranted a wedding of royal proportions. We didn't want a fuss, just a small wedding with close family and friends. We were getting married because we loved each other, not so every other fucker and the next door neighbour's cat could have a mass piss up at an expensive hotel in town. So that was fight number one. We ended up compromising and opted for a wedding not too huge but large enough to invite all the extended family my Mum wanted to impress. I'd always been a bit of a disappointment compared to my super successful cousins…even my twat of a cousin Adrian ranked higher than me on the family leader board, he was a fire fighter…a hero. That may be so but he was also an utter wanker and I was terrified he was going to volunteer to do a speech just so he could finally tell everyone about my handcuff disaster. Mum obviously saw my wedding to Archie as her chance to finally brag about me. I admit, when my cousins (apart from Adrian) were working hard for their exams, I was getting pissed on cheap vodka in a bus shelter…it's a rite of passage! I also admit, that I did get pissed at my cousin Holly's graduation party and yes I did vomit in Great Aunt Rita's hat. In my defence it was sitting on the sideboard and it did look like a large pink plant pot…if she hadn't have put it on, I probably would have got away with it. It all happened in slow motion, I remember Great Aunt Rita picking up what I thought was the plant pot and by the time it had actually registered it was her hat, there was nothing I could do…maybe laughing hysterically wasn't the best move. From that moment onwards I was officially the black sheep of the family…if my name was mentioned, the relatives would tut and shake their heads. My Mum was clearly going to savour every minute of my accent into what she perceived as 'high society'.

The second mammoth battle was over my dress. On the day Mum and I went dress shopping, she had already decided in her own head what she wanted me to choose. She had got it into her head that the size of your dress was a reflection of your wealth and status. Mum wanted me to go for a full on meringue…not just Cinderella but something so big it could be given city status. She seriously wanted me to walk up the aisle looking like a 1970's toilet roll cover. When the shop didn't have anything suitable, she wanted to contact a private dressmaker…I wanted her to go home and leave me to choose my dress in peace! By some miracle the shop assistant sussed my Mum out immediately and handed her a copy of 'Society Brides' magazine where there was not one hooped monstrosity to be seen. The word 'society' was enough for my Mum to have a complete change of mind regarding my perfect dress, elegance and simplicity were now the key components to look for...thank fuck for that! The third dress I tried on was perfect...it had a sweatheart neckline and it was fitted from top to bottom. As I turned to look at the back, I caught sight of my substantial arse and suddenly had a premonition. I was standing at the alter with Archie and as the priest asked us to kneel, I felt the dress straining against my buttocks and then suddenly, they burst free treating the whole church to the delightful sight of my butt cheeks and big knickers. Breaking into a cold sweat I took it off as quickly as I could. I wanted my wedding day to be perfect, there was no way I could risk any arse accidents. A couple of dresses later, I found it...my perfect gown. It was ivory, because let's face it, me in virginal white was never going to work. It had a fitted bodice which showed of a modest amount of cleavage and a long, floaty full skirt. The shop assistant place a veil on my head and I have to admit I felt like a princess...I felt beautiful.

The third and final 'battle of the wedding' we had was by far the biggest. Bridesmaids...fucking bridesmaids! My Mum wanted me to ask all three of my cousins from hell to be my bridesmaids;

'I can't wait to tell your Aunty Maureen you want her girls to be bridesmaids.'

'But I don't want them to be bridesmaids Mum, I would rather eat my own eyeballs.'

'Don't talk rubbish Ann, the family will expect it.'

'I don't like them, they don't like me. I don't give a shit what the family expect…it's not happening.'

To say she wasn't happy was an understatement. She flounced off and didn't speak to me for three days. Part of me did feel a bit mean. I know Mum wanted to impress the relatives but my cousins didn't even speak to me, they avoided me like the plague. I didn't want my wedding to be a circus of hypocrisy. I just wanted a lovely, truthful day where Archie and I celebrated our love and didn't bow down to the cult of Aunty Maureen and my sickeningly perfect cousins. Aunty Maureen was a formidable woman, she was my Mum's only sister and had adopted the roll of family matriarch after my Nana died. Whilst Mum was sulking, I asked my Dad to have a word with her…he normally didn't say much but could always be relied upon to be the voice of reason in a crisis;

'I've been talking with your Father and I admit, I overstepped the mark when it came to your bridesmaids. It should be your choice entirely and I respect that. Although you do realise Aunty Rita will probably write you out of her will…but that's your decision and I will say no more.'

Typical Mum, she always has to have the last word. I couldn't give a shit whether I'm in Aunty Rita's will or not. I think I was written out of it straight after the hat incident…there was no coming back from that! As for my bridesmaids…I asked my friend Veronica, along with Sylvia who was going to be my maid of honour. In keeping with Sylvia's alter ego, their dresses were flamingo pink…she was thrilled and more than a little excited that the hotel we had chosen was in the countryside.

As our wedding day approached, I was really looking forward to getting it over and done with. The initial excitement had well and truly worn off. Archie and I seemed to spend all our time talking about the wedding. Instead of having a quickie on the settee before Corrie we were talking button holes and wedding favours. The days of me giving him blow jobs whilst he tried to hold a sensible telephone conversation with his Mum were long gone. The endless planning was boring me shitless. I had no idea which flowers in the button holes I wanted to co-ordinate with my bouquet…apparently 'a red one' wasn't specific enough. For fuck's sake, I'm not Alan Titchmarsh. Finally we decided on roses…red roses as a symbol of our love. See I could 'wedding' when I put my mind to it. Archie wasn't much better. If I asked him anything relating to flowers or place settings, he would stare at me blankly. The most I could hope for was he would remember to give the rings to his best man. Archie had chosen his brother Simon, which was a huge relief as Simon was as sensible as you can get. I didn't need to worry about his speech being controversial. It would probably send the guests to sleep. Archie and I had become dull…we were wedding wankers and the sooner things got back to normal the better.

The big day dawned and all the mundane, boring shit was forgotten…I was so excited. If I could make it to the church without wetting myself I would be doing really well. I got ready at my Mum and Dad's house. Apparently it's bad luck for the bride and groom to see each other the night before the wedding…it's utter bollocks but by that point I wasn't prepared to tempt fate. Sylvia and Veronica came armed with Prosecco to help me get ready and by the time the wedding cars arrived I was already half pissed. I walked downstairs and took my Dad's hand;

'You look beautiful Ann…I'm so proud.'

That was it. My bottom lip started to wobble and my eyes welled up;

'Don't cry you silly cow…you'll ruin your make up.'

I could always rely on Veronica to bring me back down to earth. When we arrived at the church Sylvia faffed with my skirt and my veil…there was absolutely no need but she took her maid of honour duties very seriously. I ended up having to shoot her one of my death stares…for fuck's sake just let me get down the fucking aisle before Archie changes his mind. The organist started to play and Dad walked me towards the love of my life. Thankfully he looked pleased to see me…it was really going to happen! When he gently lifted the veil off my face and looked deep into my eyes my heart melted and my fanny pulsated. Suddenly Daniel's wax bellend became a distant memory and Miss Fucking Perfection Personified could fuck right off. I would never have to go roller skating or look at a dick pic ever again. I couldn't have been happier. The ceremony was everything I could have dreamed of…and thankfully the recurring nightmare I'd had of Miss Fucking Perfection Personified charging into the church heavily pregnant didn't happen. So that was me Ann without an 'e' officially a married woman. As we left the church Sylvia absolutely murdered 'Ave Maria.' She sounded like a cat fight in an alley on a Saturday night. When she offered to sing us out, she had assured me she was a trained classical singer…if she paid for the training she should definitely ask for a refund. Her singing teacher must have been deaf. You know what, it was funny and that's what I wanted for my wedding…laughter and joy.

CHAPTER TWO

The Reception

We went straight to our reception from the church. The hotel was beautiful. It was just out of town and set in acres of countryside…much to my great relief, there wasn't a swinger in sight. Champagne in hand, we greeted our guests as they entered the dining room for the wedding breakfast. I don't think I have ever shaken so many hands and I'm starting to feel like the Queen. I always wondered why they called it a wedding breakfast when I'd be getting more sausage later than there was on the menu. As we took our seats I felt like the Queen again, sitting at the top table looking down over my minions. After our sumptuous three course meal it was time for the speeches. Archie and my Dad stood up and gave the most beautiful speeches, my make up was well and truly ruined by the time they finished…never had I ever felt so loved and adored. Then it was Simon's turn, I wasn't worried at all when he began to speak. He was just going to round the speeches off, ask us to cut the cake and then   direct everyone to get pissed and dance the night away;

'Archie and Ann, didn't meet in the most conventional of ways. They first met in A&E, where their eyes met over Ann's severely swollen labia…she'd had an allergic reaction to hair remover cream. There was clearly a mutual attraction which grew with each of Ann's trips to the casualty department…I think it was handcuffs next and then love balls.'

What the fuck…did Archie not check his speech before he stood up and told everyone my most intimate secrets? As if this wasn't bad enough, my cousin Adrian took this as his cue…

'Me and a couple of the lads from the brigade had to release her!'

Our wedding guests found it hilarious but I didn't know where to look. I looked at my Mum and she glared at me. Then I smiled sweetly at Archie's Mum and she shot me a stare which said 'the minute we're out of here, I'm speaking to Archie about getting an annulment.' The rest of his speech thankfully passed without controversy and the guests seemed happy to toast our future happiness. Archie kept apologising and our Mothers kept glaring. They started staring at each other so intensely at one point I was seriously concerned they were going to end up brawling beneath the ice statue. Cutting the cake was slightly awkward, we smiled for the pictures and made sure we didn't leave the knife anywhere near either of our Mothers. Job done, I necked back a couple of glasses of champagne and started to feel much more relaxed. So much so, that when we it was time to take the party to the ballroom. I grabbed Archie and pulled him into the nearest toilet. We were both well up for it after the sex drought we'd endured whilst planning the wedding. Both pissed, we stumbled into a cubicle and shut the door. Archie pushed me against the wall, hitched up my skirt and fucked me harder and harder, with each thrust he called out my name;

'Oh Archie, I love it when you say my name in a high pitched voice.'

He stopped and we looked at each other in horror…'that wasn't me Ann'. Neither of us wanted to look but knew we had to…It was my Great Aunt Rita. We hadn't locked the fucking door!

'Ann, the DJ is calling for you and Archie to do the first dance…if you want to carry on I think I can buy you an extra five minutes.'

With that, she turned around and walked out. Archie and I looked at each other and laughed. The moment had well and truly been lost but good old Great Aunt Rita! She was waiting at the door when we entered the ballroom, she gave me a cheeky wink and patted Archie on the arse…maybe I wasn't going to be written out of her will after all.

We both avoided making eye contact with our Mothers as we headed to the dance floor to kick the evening off with our first dance. Archie gently took me into his arms and the spotlight shone on us as we waited for the music to start…this was our iconic moment, it was just me and Archie wrapped up in our love for each other. It was going to be perfect and would be captured for eternity on our wedding video. I'd chosen 'Up where we belong' from An Officer and A Gentleman as our song. I absolutely hated the film…Richard Gere was fit but that whole concept that a woman needed a man to give them a better life was sick inducing, but I loved the song so I had to forget my feminist principles for five minutes. As the music started I looked deeply into Archie's eyes because love really was lifting us up where we belonged. Unfortunately I didn't get the beautiful, romantic piano introduction I was waiting for. We were greeted with 'Say oops upside your head'…what the actual fuck? Then I remembered, when I was talking to the DJ about our first dance I couldn't remember the name of the song so I asked him for the 'Up' song that was popular at parties. Shit, fuck, bollocks…The Gap Band it was. All eyes were on us so we just had to go with the flow… we immediately sat on the floor and started singing along and dancing whilst gesturing to our guests to join us. Soon more or less everyone in the room and joined our train on the floor. The notable exceptions were our Mothers and Aunty Maureen who tutted and shook their heads as even Great Aunt Rita sang along at the top of her mercilessly out of tune voice. It was such fun…much better than that romantic shite. Unfortunately my Mum didn't feel the same way and the minute we got off the dance floor she grabbed me for a bollocking;

'Ann, you really need to tone it down. What with all that talk about your nether regions in the speeches and now this. It's unbecoming Ann. You are a doctor's wife now and you need to behave and stop embarrassing yourself.'

Now that was taking it a bit too fucking far. I would embarrass myself as much as I wanted! This was my wedding day and no one, particularly my own Mother was going to piss on my bonfire;

'You do realise doctors are human Mum…they are not mythical God like beings to be worshipped but normal flesh and blood humans that like a laugh as much as the next person. It's not the 1950's, things have moved on and I am not going to live my life like I'm in an episode of Call the Midwife.'

I didn't want to fall out with her so I kissed her on the cheek and as I walked off she yet again had to have the last word;

'You need to be more like Sylvia...she's a model of decorum, a real lady.'

Ha, ha, ha, ha...if only she knew Sylvia had had more cocks than the local chicken farm. She was less decorum and more dickorum! I walked away giggling to myself. I couldn't say anything about Sylvia...I would never betray her trust.

After my conversation with my Mum I realised that I hadn't actually seen Sylvia for ages...I asked Archie if he knew where she was and he thought he had seen her heading towards the main doors of the hotel. I decided to pop outside and see if she was about...it was also a good opportunity to have a crafty smoke whilst Archie was chatting to his friends. I went outside and hid behind a wall whilst I sparked up. After a couple of puffs, I heard rustling coming from the bushes. Shit…could it be a cow? I don't have a particularly good history with cows…they don't like me and I'm not exactly keen on their cow patting, ear licking ways. I keep perfectly still…if it doesn't notice me it might just wander off. The rustling gets louder and closer until Sylvia bursts through the bushes still wearing her flamingo mask and adjusting her dress;

'Sylvia! What the fuck are you doing?'

'Do you really have to ask Ann? You know me…if I see an opportunity, I'll make the most of it! Whilst I've got you on your own. I just wanted to say how proud I am to be your friend. I hope you and Archie will be very happy together and I can't tell you how much I regret how awful I was to you when you were seeing Josh…if things had been different you could have been part of my family. Anyway, I need to get back inside so I'd better put the flamingo away for another day.'

I laughed out loud as she put the mask in her bag and made her way inside as if nothing had happened…I loved

Sylvia and I was just as proud to have her as my friend. Just as I was starting to reminisce about how much she hated me when we first met, the bushes started to rustle again. It was starting to feel like a horror film where the unwitting victim is lulled into a false sense of security before they are attacked by a killer cow from hell. This time a larger figure burst through the bushes and I'm sorry to say I screamed like a girl. Strangely the figure screamed back…it was my cousin Adrian. What the fuck was going on…surely he wasn't with Sylvia? He's half her age…no he couldn't have been, could he?

'Adrian, you knob. What the fuck are you doing.'

All the colour had drained from his face and he looked like he had seen a ghost as he spluttered;

'Same as you Ann. I nipped out for a crafty fag. Why, what do you think I was doing?'

I decide to just come out with it;

'I thought you might have been shagging Sylvia?'

'Who the fuck is Sylvia? Honestly you've always had an active imagination…anyway shouldn't you be inside doing wedding shit?'

There was something seriously suss about the whole thing, but he was right I should have been inside with my gorgeous husband.

I went back inside and we spent the rest of the evening laughing, dancing and thanking our guests for sharing our day. After the telling off my Mum gave me, I purposely asked the DJ to play all the popular, interactive party tunes. You name it, we did it: YMCA, Superman, Time Warp and even to my deep shame…The Birdie Song. Fuelled with love, adrenaline and lots of champagne I gave every song my absolute all…my Mother looked like she was going to combust. I might have been imagining it but when we danced to the Time Warp, Adrian and Sylvia gave each other a knowing look when they did 'the pelvic thrust'. I swear he winked and she licked her lips…something was going on and I would eventually get to the bottom of it. As the evening finally drew to a end I was absolutely exhausted but I couldn't have been happier. I was Ann and I may not have had an extra 'e' but I had a fucking husband!! Archie somehow managed to carry me over the threshold of our hotel room and we both collapsed onto the bed. After a long and wonderful day we were absolutely knackered, even my fanny was too tired to tingle as he kissed me goodnight. This was the start of the rest of our lives together and I had never been happier.

CHAPTER THREE

Now I wasn't expecting that!

It's been a couple of weeks since Archie and I got back from our honeymoon and I'm pleased to say we are more loved up than ever. After our perfectly joyous wedding, we spent two weeks in a luxury resort in Marbella. It was no expense spared and thankfully paid for by Archie's parents...I was half expecting them to cancel it after Simon revealed my fanny troubles in his speech. It was absolutely beautiful, two whole weeks of enjoying the sun, the sea and each other...not necessarily in that order and on one occasion we enjoyed all three at the same time. We had spent most of the day enjoying the hotel pool and were particularly enjoying the cocktails from the poolside bar...never a good combination. It started off innocently enough...Archie was picking me up and throwing me into the water, I was splashing him. We were just arsing around in the pool until I jumped into his arms and he kissed me...my fanny tingled like it had never tingled before and Archie was nearly popping out of his swimming trunks. We were desperate for each other and a quickie was called for but we were in the middle of the swimming pool so it wasn't going to happen. Until that is, Archie pointed out the stone waterfall...we could go behind there and no one would see us...result! We hid ourself away behind the waterfall and had the most amazing, frantic sex. I was completely lost in the moment and as I came, I heard cheers and whistles. They sounded so real and I was amazed by the intensity of my orgasm until I realised...they were real! We hadn't noticed that the stone waterfall was open to one side so we had a rather amused audience...oh for fuck's sake! The lifeguards were blowing their whistles, pointing at us and one was holding up a rather large yellow card...I later learnt this was a warning, one more misdemeanour and we could be asked to leave the hotel. They couldn't have drawn more attention to us if they tried...twats. We couldn't get out of the pool quickly enough and had to do the walk of shame past cheering holiday makers...a couple of the blokes patted Archie on the back and shook his hand. The women were less forgiving and when they weren't looking lustfully at Archie they were looking at me in disgust. Thankfully we were flying home the next day so we wouldn't have to see any of new found fan club again...ever!

I keep looking at my wedding ring. I still can't believe it actually happened...I managed to bag Dr Gorgeous and he's mine forever. The only thing that's putting a dampener on it, is I've been feeling fucking awful for the past few days. I'm so tired and I feel horribly sick, so sick I can't even face a crafty smoke so it must be bad. Maybe I picked up some tropical disease on honeymoon...can you actually catch a tropical disease in Spain? I quickly type 'tired and sick after honeymoon' into Dr Google (I know I'm married to an actual doctor but I don't want to worry him) and nearly every search result says the same thing... PREGNANT. Oh fuck off,

I'm not having that. We did dispense with contraception just before our wedding but it takes ages to get pregnant…doesn't it? Thinking about it, my period is late but to be honest they were never particularly regular so I didn't think anything of it. I also have a splendid pair of tits, they are much fuller than normal, but that's down to all the cake I stuffed my face with on honeymoon…right? This really is starting to look like Archie's little swimmers hit the jackpot. I've got a spare pregnancy test upstairs…we had a scare a few months ago and if I remember I've still got one test left. I empty the bathroom cupboards in a frenzy of dread and excitement and finally find the lone pregnancy test. Making sure to read the instructions carefully I pee on the stick and wait. I don't have to wait too long…there's a line, a bright unmistakeable line. Which means I'm preggo, up the duff, with child…fucking hell! I immediately get on the phone to Veronica;

'Vron…I'm pregnant.'

'Did you do a test?'

'I did and I've got a line, a big fuck off blue line.'

'Do another one or two and call me back,'

That was my Veronica, blunt and to the point. There was no messing with her, she was fiercely practical and I suppose she did have a point. It was perfectly feasible that the test was giving me a false positive.

I throw on my coat and head down to the local pharmacy. When I get there, there is a huge queue, typical, there's never usually a queue…it must be pension day as everyone in there appears to be over 80. I can't wait and find myself waving the test at the woman behind the counter;

'Yoo hoo! Is this positive?'

She's looking at me like I'm deranged;

'I can't tell from here, you'll have to join the queue and I'll get to you when I can.'

I join the back of the queue to much tutting and shaking of heads from the other customers. It takes forever for it to move and I now know all about Mrs Smith's corns, Mrs Robinson's waterworks and Mrs Henderson's piles…frighteningly this is the future! I eventually get to the counter and the pharmacist does indeed confirm my test is positive. Just to be sure I buy four more and run home like Charlie with his golden ticket. Once home I squeeze out every last drop of pee to do the four tests in quick succession. Everyone is positive, so I guess that's it…I'm officially pregnant. Clearly it's a bit of a shocker, but I think I'm excited…yes I'm definitely excited! I'm expecting Baby Gorgeous and I can't wait until their eighteenth birthday when I can tell them they were conceived in a swimming pool.   What the fuck do I do now?   How big am I actually going to get? How the actual fuck am I going to squeeze something the size of a melon out of something the size of a pea?   What will become of my poor foof? How am I going to tell Archie?   I quickly jump online and search 'pregnancy reveal.' I wish I hadn't, it's all balloons, gift boxes and confetti. I feel too sick to go back to the shops so I'll have to use what I can find in the house.   After searching for all of five minutes all I can find is a skanky piece of left over Christmas wrapping paper…oh well that will have to do.   I wrap up all the pregnancy tests and wait for Archie to get home.

Time passes really, really slowly as I wait for Archie to get home, so I try and pass the time online. I resist the temptation to buy maternity pants and booties and settle with ordering a couple of pregnancy books. I wanted to know everything...or maybe I didn't? After what feels like the entire length of a pregnancy I hear Archie's car pulling into the drive. I run to the front door and as he steps out of his car I thrust the packaged tests into his hand;

'Archie, I have a surprise for you...open it!'

He looks confused;

'Just ignore the Christmas paper and open it.'

This was taking longer than I had hoped. Archie opens the package as he walks into the house and it takes him a few seconds to register what the tests are telling him;

'These are pregnancy tests Ann...and they're positive...I'm going to be a Dad?'

With that he started dancing around the living room singing 'I'm going to be a Daddy' over and over again.

Safe to say he was just as excited as I was. We sat down and began to chat about what the baby would look like…would it have my curly hair and Archie's devilish good looks? Or horror of horror would it be a genetic throwback and be the spitting image of my cousin Adrian? After discussing every possible hair/eye combination, we eventually we got around to names;

'In my family Ann, it's traditional that all children born are named after relatives two generations away from their parent.'

I quickly try and work out what two generations away from Archie would be and can't for the life of me figure it out…I blame my pregnancy brain;

'So that leaves us with Edgar for a boy and Phyllis for a girl.'

You have got to be fucking joking…Edgar or Phyliss. He looks deadly serious and my stomach lurches as I realise he's not joking. Sorry Archie, you may be the love of my life but that's not going to happen. I don't give a shit if it's a family tradition dating back to the dawn of time. There is no way I am saddling my children with those names…no way…not happening…ever! I knew better than anyone how important a child's name was. If my parents had only given me that extra 'e' I would have been 'Mary' in the school nativity play rather than' third donkey to the left.' My whole career path would have been completely different. I would have worn head scarves and worked in publishing…I would have been respected, maybe even thought of as regal. That said. If things had been different, I might not have met Archie and I could have ended up with a boring old fart who wanted to name our children Tarquinius and Fenella;

'I'm sorry Archie. Much as I love you, I'm putting my foot well and truly down. I know old names have become fashionable, but not those old names.'

His face dropped and he actually looked quite sad. Well tough shit…family tradition would well and truly take a back seat if it saved my child from a lifetime of having the piss taken out of it.

'My Mum is going to be so disappointed…are you sure you don't like them?'

Am I sure? Is the Pope a Catholic?

'It obviously means a lot to you, so I'll compromise and we'll give the baby Edgar or Phyllis as a middle name.'

He looked happier and I felt like I had averted a crisis...seriously, I always thought I should have worked for The United Nations. As for our child's middle name, as soon as they were old enough I would just tell them not to use it...Edgar and Phyllis would soon become a distant memory.

We decided we weren't going to tell anyone about my pregnancy until got to 12 weeks. It was going to be our wonderful secret and for a short time it would just be me, Archie and Baby Gorgeous. I'll just have to disguise my nausea the best I can and feed everyone the line I've got a stomach bug. Archie has got his doctor's head on and is currently in the kitchen throwing away anything I shouldn't eat or drink during my pregnancy...bye Prosecco, cheerio caffeinated coffee, laters soft cheese, ta ta dry roasted peanuts. From now on nothing would cross my lips unless it was good for the baby...chocolate is good in pregnancy isn't it? How did I get so lucky? I almost can't believe that I've gone from being a boiler of bellends who had resigned herself to a life of cat rescue

to a married, pregnant woman...how very grown up of
me.

CHAPTER FOUR

12 Weeks

The past few weeks have passed in a haze of nausea and tiredness. Why the fuck do they call it morning sickness? I've felt sick morning, noon and night…just feeling sick in the morning would be a luxury at this point. I feel like there's nothing that hasn't made me feel sick. Unfortunately that includes Archie's cock, so our sex life has been virtually non-existent. My fanny hasn't tingled for ages…I think she's protesting against what she knows is coming. Then there's the tiredness…why am I so tired? I'm in bed with at 9pm with a cup of cocoa most evenings and if I watch anything of TV that's remotely happy or even the slightest bit sad I can't stop the tears coming. I've been to see my GP and I've booked in with the Midwife. I have a folder containing my notes so I'm all official. Nobody close to me seems to have figured out I'm pregnant yet…how I've managed to keep it a secret I really don't know. I've wanted to shout it from the roof tops. I want to tell the world I'm going to be a Mummy, a Mum, a Mummage or when the baby gets older I could be really trendy and just tell it call me Ann. Today we've reached out first milestone and are going for our 12 week scan. I'm beyond excited… I get to see Baby Gorgeous (according to my books, baby is now fully formed and is about the size of a plum). Then once that's done, we've got the family and Sylvia coming over for a meal and we'll tell them all the good news then. Archie is doing the cooking, nothing too exciting just a lasagne…but I just couldn't. Even thinking about the smell of cooking is making me heave. I'm convinced I've got the tiniest of tiny baby bumps, my clothes are starting to feel a little tight around the waist. However, I could just be imagining it because I am so desperate to be huge and that is something I'd never thought I'd hear myself say.

I'm waiting for Archie outside the hospital when I suddenly feel tap on my shoulder. I turn round and it's Sylvia…it's lovely to see her but I don't want to blow my cover when we are slow close to making our announcement tonight;

'Ann, what are you doing here?'

Shit, shit what do I say?

'I'm meeting my gorgeous husband for lunch lovely, are you all set for tonight?'

She doesn't seem convinced…Sylvia can smell a rat from a mile away.

'Oh…meeting him outside the maternity unit, why not outside A&E. Surely that would be easier given he's working in there…or is there something you're not telling me?'

Oh for fuck's sake she's sussed me and I can tell she's not going to let it drop.

'Ok, ok…I'll tell you but you mustn't tell anyone. I'm pregnant and we're going in for my 12 week scan. Nobody knows Sylvia, so please, please don't say anything.'

Sylvia lets out a scream and immediately envelopes me in an enormous bear hug. The smell of her perfume immediately makes me start to gag and I have to gently push her away as she offers her congratulations;

'I knew it. I knew you were pregnant…you never refuse a Prosecco and the times we've met up and you haven't popped outside for a crafty fag. You also look like shit…hope you don't mind me saying. I take it you're going to tell everyone tonight and that's what the dinner party is all about?'

Well I wouldn't call it a dinner party…bollocks, will they all think it's a dinner party? I'd better send Archie out for a Viennetta later;

'Can't pull the wool over your eyes Sylvia can I? Yes, we're going to tell everyone tonight. So remember you know nothing…look Archie is coming so I'd better go. Remember, not a word to anyone.'

As I walk over to Archie I can see Sylvia out of the corner of my eye winking at him and giving him the thumbs up…it's going to be all around the hospital by tea-time isn't it? Archie kisses me on the cheek and is clearly confused by Sylvia's behaviour;

'What's wrong with Sylvia…why is she winking at me?'

'She's probably pleased to you.'

'I just saw her 5 minutes ago…what is she doing? It looks like she's gesturing at my crotch and giving the thumbs up.'

Oh for fuck's sake Sylvia, she couldn't have made it more obvious if she tried. I manage to pull Archie into the maternity unit out of Sylvia's line of sight and once we see the Ultrasound Department all thoughts of Sylvia are forgotten.

The waiting room looks empty which I'm hoping means we won't have to wait too much longer. I had to drink so much water in preparation for the scan I literally feel like I am going to wet myself any second. As we take our seats I notice a couple in the corner. They both have their heads buried in magazines but I'd recognise them anywhere…bloody hell, universe, what are you playing at. There's literally nowhere to hide and I take a sharp intake of breath as Ryan looks up and taps Miss Fucking Perfection Personified on the thigh. Ryan almost seems pleased to see me. Less so Camilla whose plumped up lips just about manage to form a half smile when she registers who I am;

'Hi Ann, no need to ask what you're doing here.'

Why the fuck is he speaking to me like we are long lost friends? The last time I saw him he was giving that delightful woman a good seeing to, why on earth would I even want to acknowledge him? Archie looks confused;

'Oh do you two know each other?'

Before I can answer Miss Fucking Perfection Personified chips in;

'Ann used to date Ryan…before he met me. So, what do they call you sweetie?'

How fucking brazen? She's looking Archie straight in the eyes and fluttering her particularly long, false eyelashes at him. Even in the first trimester of pregnancy she's immaculately coiffured and I start to feel insecure. She's all glossy hair, tits and teeth and I just look fucked after three months of throwing up. I needn't have worried, Archie clearly has the measure of her;

'All I can say is Ryan's loss is absolutely my gain.'

Ha! Shove that up your perfectly groomed and probably bleached arse! Before she can open her mouth to respond, she's called through for her scan. She waves coquettishly at Archie as she walks off. Ryan simply nods and for a split second I feel sorry for him. He looks deflated, defeated and like he has the weight of the world on his shoulders…serves him fucking right! Vile though she is, the lovely Camilla actually did me a favour. If she hadn't stolen Ryan from me I would never have dated Archie and I wouldn't be sitting here now. Archie seems distinctly unimpressed;

'Who the hell was that dreadful woman?'

I should have felt comforted by the fact he thought she was dreadful but my hormones kick in;

'Her name is Camilla but I call her Miss Fucking Perfection Personified. For some reason before I met you she was stalking my love life…kept cropping up where I least expected her to. So please Archie, if you ever get bored of me, promise me now that you won't find yourself in her clearly waxed arms.'

Shit, Archie looks a bit hurt;

'You're being silly Ann. When I married you I meant every word of the vows I made in church. Its you and me forever. You are beautiful, you are funny, you are my wife and you are growing our baby. Why would I want anyone else when you are perfection personified to me.'

Ha, double fuck you Camilla! No amount of batting your false eyelashes at Archie is going to turn his head…you lost! Archie kisses me on the forehead and my fanny finally starts to tingle just as we are called through for the scan.

I lie down on the bed and Archie sits beside me holding my hand. The sonographer runs through some details and then asks me to undo my jeans. She tucks a paper towel into my knickers and squeezes some fucking freezing cold gel on my lower tummy. The screen is turned towards us as she starts to scan. Within seconds we see it, the grainy black and white image of Baby Gorgeous. Our little squidge is wriggling about, obviously pissed off at being disturbed…that's my boy or girl. I look at Archie and the soft git is crying…that starts me off and we are both staring at the screen with tears of joy running down our faces. Who would've thought a quick shag in a hotel swimming pool could have created something so beautiful. The sonographer takes some measurements and I am approximately 12 weeks and 5 days pregnant…so that's nearly 13 weeks which means I've only got another 27 weeks to go! I do ask if the sonographer can tell what sex the baby is, but it's too early to tell and we'll have to wait for the 20 week scan, if we want to know that is. The baby looks healthy and everything is progressing how it should be and that's good enough for me. I blow a kiss at my little squidge as the sonographer finishes the scan and once she's done, she hands me a paper towel so I can wipe away the gel…that stuff gets everywhere! We leave the room floating on air, clasping our treasured first scan picture of Baby Gorgeous. I'm brought back down to earth with a bump by my bulging bladder;

'Shit, Archie. I can't tell you how much I need to pee…I think I'm dribbling!'

The waiting room had filled up since we left and the excited baby chatter turns to silence as just about everyone in the room turns to look at us. I left Archie to smile and nod knowingly at the largely sympathetic audience I had attracted, whilst I dived into the nearest toilet. The relief once I was done…I can't tell you!

Archie quickly ushered me out of the doors and once we were back in the car we just sat and looked at our precious picture. We are both lost in the moment and are rudely awakened by Sylvia hammering on the car window. She's gesticulating wildly again and Archie finally twigs that she knows about the baby;

'She knows doesn't she?'

'I'm sorry Archie. She guessed and there's no arguing with her when she thinks she's right.'

I wind down the car window and Sylvia excitedly snatches the scan picture out of my hand;

'How beautiful, congratulations you two. You're very naughty Archie trying to keep it a secret from me. Don't worry, I haven't told anyone.'

As if by magic, my phone pinged with a message from Stacey AKA Little Miss Smug Bitch…congratulating me an Archie on our baby news. We both shouted 'Sylvia' in unison;

'Well when I said I didn't tell anyone, it was just Stacey and maybe a couple of the nurses in A&E, oh and Bill the porter…they're all thrilled for you.'

So as predicted she had told the whole hospital…if she could just keep quiet for the rest of the day we might have chance of the family not finding out. As she leaves us to finish her shift she absolutely promises not to say another word. For some reason I'm not convinced as walks off zipping her lips. Today had been a good day. Baby Gorgeous was healthy, strong and doing all the right things.   Archie absolutely did not fancy Miss Fucking Perfection Personified and Sylvia had saved us the job of telling Archie's colleagues about the baby. I was really looking forward to breaking the news to our families. I know my side of the family will be thrilled…My Mum was going to be beside herself. Not only had her daughter married a doctor she was now having his child. Archie's Mum however may insist on an exorcism once the baby is born…her first Grandchild and it could be just like me!

CHAPTER FIVE

Time to tell the family

As soon as we arrive home from the hospital Archie starts cooking. I've retreated to the sofa with a large bottle of ginger beer. Ginger is supposed to help with morning sickness but I've drunk gallons of the stuff and it hasn't made much of a difference. It taste good though...maybe it's my first craving?   We're going to have quite a houseful tonight. My parents, Archie's parents, Sylvia, Aunty Maureen and strangely my cousin Adrian.   My Mum called earlier to tell me he really wanted to come which is fucking strange. He's definitely up to something as he's always the first to give family meals the swerve. I could be generous and say he doesn't want his Mum to be on her own but he doesn't usually give a shit. I'm only thankful his sisters the 'perfect' cousins were too busy being perfect to come. Our news would have been overshadowed by their latest career successes...'I know she's the new CEO of a multi-national company but I'm having a baby.' The thought makes me feel queasy again and I take a huge slurp of ginger beer. I'm sure all will be revealed later…he probably wants to bring up the wedding speeches again so he can watch me squirm in front of Archie's Mum. To be honest I'm really not arsed. Tonight is our night…me, Archie and baby gorgeous and nothing is going take the shine off our announcement. Just as I'm about to nod off I suddenly realise…we don't have a starter! This is the first time Archie's parents have visited us as a married couple and they can't not have a starter…they'd think even less of me than they do already. I send Archie to the corner shop to pick up a few cans of cream of tomato soup. Disaster averted we're all set…cream of tomato soup to start, lasagne for the main course and Viennetta and squirty cream for desert. It's not going to win us any Michelin stars but fuck it…it's going to be warm and tasty. If they don't like it they'll have to get a takeaway on the way home.

The doorbell rings and our first guest has arrived. I open the door to Sylvia who is holding the biggest teddy bear I think I have ever seen…she's not exactly subtle. Is she?

'I couldn't resist, the baby will love it.'

I get Archie to hide it upstairs before anyone else arrives and explain to Sylvia once again that the family don't know so she has to keep quiet…for an incredibly intelligent woman Sylvia is really fucking stupid at times. I give her a glass of Prosecco and decide to keep her close so I can shut her up if she starts to spill the beans. Archie's parents arrive next…his Mum air kisses me on both cheeks and then completely ignores me as she makes a beeline for her son. His Dad who is a man of few words, pats me on the shoulder and gives me a friendly nod. Finally my parents, Aunty Maureen and Adrian arrive. Adrian catches Sylvia's eye as soon as he walks in and I'm sure I can feel some sort of tension between them…surely not? It must be my pregnancy brain playing tricks on me again. Sylvia is old enough to be Adrian's Mother. So far so good, we are all in the living room enjoying a glass of Prosecco except me. I'm on orange juice which doesn't escape Archie's Mum;

'Are you not having a glass of wine Ann?'

I say the first thing that comes into my head;

'No, not tonight…I'm on antibiotics.'

I should have guessed she wouldn't leave it there;

'Oh dear…nothing serious I hope?'

Before I can answer, Sylvia pipes up;

'She's got a water infection.'

A fucking water infection…of all the things she could have said, she had to say that. Archie's Mum looks typically disgusted and she immediately turns her back on me. In an attempt to change the subject Archie invites everyone to take a seat at the table. Once our guests are all seated I serve the starter…the Mother-in-Law from hell takes one taste and her eyes narrow. She's sussed it's Happy Shopper soup and I haven't actually used the blender she bought us as a wedding present;

'Did you make this soup, Ann?'

What a loaded question…the evil witch;

'No, I didn't. Archie has done all the cooking today…I'm a lucky lady.'

With that her whole tone changed...the soup was delicious, a culinary triumph and he'd have to give her the recipe. Believe me I would love to tell her to fuck right off but she's Archie's Mum and I have to give her a chance. After all, Sylvia hated me when she first met me and now we are best friends. Once we have finished our soup there's a slight delay before the main course so Sylvia pops outside to get some fresh air. Not long after she goes out Adrian gets up and gestures to me that he's going outside for a smoke. I'm starting to wonder whether Sylvia is a secret smoker and Adrian is facilitating it...now that makes more sense. Thankfully everyone seems to be getting on well and Aunty Maureen is loving every minute of telling Archie's Mum how wonderfully successful her daughter's are. She's even bigging Adrian up, the heroic firefighter who risks his life everyday...I can't compete and I don't fucking want to! Just as dinner is ready to be served we hear a large crash coming from the shed outside. We ignore initially as it's probably just cats, but then we hear it again and again...could it be burglars or Camilla come to snatch Archie away by any means necessary? Archie leads the ways and we all head outside to see what's going on. It's dark, but we can see shadows and I'm convinced I saw a flash of pink. As we quietly make our way to the shed we can hear grunting. Archie switches on the outside light which bathes the shed in brightness and he bravely kicks the door open. I was expecting cats or maybe even foxes but my eye will never unsee the sight that greeted us all...Adrian was up to his nuts in Sylvia's guts. Naturally wearing her flamingo mask, she was bent across the work surface and Adrian was giving her a damn good seeing to from behind. They were completely in the spotlight and nothing was left to the imagination...I will never be able to unsee the sight of Adrian's bare arse...the was light bouncing off it like moonbeams. They were so caught up in the moment it took them a couple of seconds to register they had an audience. Adrian tried desperately to pull his trousers up managing to fall flat on his face in the process. Sylvia appeared unfazed as she simply smoothed her dress down, stepped over Adrian and headed back towards the house. Aunty Maureen was fuming!

'Adrian, what the hell do you think you are doing…never in my life have I been so embarrassed. Who is the woman in the mask…come here you!'

With that she grabbed Sylvia from behind, span her round and pulled the flamingo mask off;

'You…but, but you're old enough to be his Mother.'

Sylvia seems a bit stung by this but is having none of it;

'Age is a number…Adrian is in his thirties. I'm in my early sixties and we are both consenting adults. You should be happy your son has bagged himself a cougar. I think we need to leave Ady and let your Mum come to terms with us being a couple.'

They're a couple…well fucking hell, that's a revelation. Adrian finally managed to pull up his trousers, hauled himself up from the floor and they walked out hand in hand. I knew they were up to no good at my wedding and that's why he wanted to come here tonight…to see Sylvia. He must be well smitten if he's prepared to put up with an evening with his family. As we head back into the house I don't know what to say;

'Who'd have thought Adrian would be shagging Sylvia?'

'I wonder if he gets her in a fireman's lift?'

'Does she ever take that fucking mask off?'

None of these feel appropriate so I decide the best course of action is to keep my mouth shut. I serve the main course and there's not much conversation at the table as we eat. I have to stop myself from bursting out laughing as I think about Sylvia walking off cool as anything. My Mum keeps shooting me the 'don't you dare' look as she pats a still mortified Aunty Maureen on the hand. Archie's Mother is clearly horrified and if my fanny misdemeanours weren't enough to put her off me and my family, the sight of Adrian taking Sylvia from behind has certainly done the job. The final insult for Archie's Mum comes when we serve pudding…what exactly is wrong with Viennetta and squirty cream? She looks at me like I've just served her shit on a plate and I don't think she's ever used squirty cream in her life. I think now might be a good time to announce our news…I stand up and Archie comes over and gently puts his arm around my waist;

'Thank you all for coming this evening…it's certainly been interesting and quite unexpected. Anyway, the reason we asked you all to come is because we have some news we wanted to share with you…we're having a baby!'

Everyone jumps up from the table and immediately offers their congratulations…my Mum looks like she is going to cry and even Archie's parents crack a smile. The scan picture is passed from person to person when it gets to Archie's Mum, she starts to tear up a little;

'How beautiful…it looks just like Archie when he was a foetus.'

What the actual fuck…did I hear that right? How can she remember what Archie looked like when he was a foetus? I'm starting to think she might be a bit over the top where Archie is concerned…no wonder he only let me meet her a couple of times before the wedding. Clearly this baby was going to be nothing to do with me at all…it would have Archie's eyes, Archie's hair, Archie's intelligence. For fuck's sake she is probably going to credit him with giving birth to it! We are asked the usual questions about the babies due date and if we would prefer a girl or a boy and it's all going well until my Dad asks us if we have thought of any names yet. Before we can open our mouths, Archie's Mum jumps straight in;

'Oh they don't need to think about any names. It's tradition in our family to name their children after relatives two generations removed. So this baby will be called Phyliss or Edgar.'

Well my Dad couldn't contain himself and burst out laughing;

'You can't call a child Phyliss…and Edgar's not much better.'

I kick Archie under the table and he winces…he needs to put a stop to this now before his Mum starts getting personalised baby grows printed;

'Actually Mum. We've decided to break with tradition and choose our own names for the baby…we'll use Phyllis or Edgar as a middle name.'

Oh dear…she's not happy!

'We'll discuss this in private Archie…you know how important family tradition is and I'm not letting you deviate from it just to keep her happy.'

The cheeky mare. Who does she think she is…the fucking Queen? Archie's Dad sinks into his chair and Archie jumps up from the table like my knight in shining armour.

'Sorry Mum but who is 'her?' if you are referring to Ann she's my wife and we will decide what we name our children, not you or some random cousin three times removed on Great Uncle Neville's side of the family. This is our decision and there will be no discussion in private or any other time.'

Archie's Mum doesn't respond…she grabs her bag and her coat and heads for the door dutifully followed by Archie's Dad who mouths an apology as they leave. This is the cue for my parents and Aunty Maureen to go. My Mum is so excited she's rattling on about bootees and matinee sets as she heads out of the door…what even is a matinee set? I do feel a bit sorry for Aunty Maureen…she went out for a family meal with the golden boy only to very publicly catch him shagging a near OAP. I wouldn't want to be in Adrian's shoes when he gets home. When they've all gone, Archie and I slump knackered onto the sofa…it's been quite a day. We saw our beautiful baby for the first time, caught Adrian and Sylvia copulating in our garden shed and then there was Phyllisgate…I'm not sure Archie's Mum will come round to the idea of us naming the baby ourselves but we'll cross that bridge when we come to it.

CHAPTER SIX

Sylvia and Adrian

It's been a week since the dinner party that turned into an episode of League of Gentlemen. My Mum is literally calling me on the hour every hour. She wants to know if I'm ok and if I'm eating properly? Today she actually asked me if my bowel movements were regular…that's crossing the line Mother, crossing the line. We've heard absolutely nothing from Archie's Mum which isn't a surprise really…she was fuming. Even Sylvia has been uncharacteristically quiet…Archie said she's barely spoken to him at work and she seems to have reverted to the Sylvia I first met…bad tempered and intolerant of everyone including her patients. On a much brighter note. I'm starting to feel much better…the nausea has really improved and I even managed to wake Archie up with a good morning blow job yesterday. He'd gone without for so long he went into work with a spring in his step and a smile on his face. My appetite is starting to come back and I'm partial to a packet or three of beef Monster Munch. I managing much better at work...running to the loo every time someone brought food into the office was starting to get a bit wearing and now my colleagues know I'm pregnant they are much more sympathetic. I definitely have the tiniest of baby bumps...I'm not imagining it and it won't be long until I have to start buying some maternity clothes. I'm actually so excited at the prospect of buying maternity knickers...that's not right is it?

I'm just thinking about what to make for tea and there's a knock at the door...I'm not expecting anyone and Archie is working late so I'm more than surprised to answer the door to my cousin Adrian;

'Hi Cuz. I could really do with a chat if that's ok?'

'Cuz'...what the actual fuck? He's never referred to me as 'Cuz' before and to be honest I'm glad because it's a bit cringe. I invite him in. To be honest, I'm really curious. What could he possibly want to talk to me about?

'Right, so you know that night at yours where you all caught me with Sylvia?'

'You were shagging her in my garden shed Adrian.

'Yeah, I know and I'm sorry about that but we just couldn't help ourselves. It started on the night of your wedding. We'd been checking each other out all day and then when I went outside for a cigarette she appeared from nowhere. She was wearing her flamingo mask and beckoned me into the bushes...it was seriously the best sex I had ever had.'

I think we might be getting into the realms of too much information here. I knew they were up to no good at my wedding. All that bullshit he gave me about having a cigarette...the lying twat.

'I don't know what it was about her but she sent electricity coursing through my body every time I looked at her. We saw each other virtually every day from your wedding until the other night...the sex has been phenomenal but it's not just that. We talk, we really talk. I know she's older than me, but I don't care. You would never think she's as old as she is...I have difficulty keeping up with her. She's wild Ann. Before all this kicked off we went for a drink out in the countryside one evening. On the way back we pulled into secluded lane and she did things to me that I didn't know existed! When we'd finished I stepped out of the car for a smoke and we were surrounded by bikers. We had unwittingly parked up right in the middle of their meeting place. Sylvia wasn't bothered one little bit, she got out of the car and asked them if they wanted to join in…that's something else I love bout her, her sense of humour.'

That sounded just like Sylvia and I didn't have the heart to tell him she probably wasn't joking;

'I have never felt the same way about any woman as I do about Sylvia…I think I love her Ann. When we left your house that evening, she let me take her home, kissed me on the doorstep and hasn't answered any of my calls or texts since. I need your help…I don't want to lose her. Please can you talk to her…tell her how I feel. My Mum is raging but I don't care what anyone thinks…I just want to be with her.'

Well. I wasn't expecting that. He's got it really bad…he actually loves her. I don't know how to break it to him that Sylvia is not the settling down type and just as I'm about to tell him he probably needs to put Sylvia behind him, there's another knock at the door. I look out of the window and bloody hell…it's Sylvia. What do I do now? I tell Adrian to go and hide upstairs and let her in. She gives me a big hug as soon as I open the door and apologises for not getting in touch;

'I'm so sorry for not calling you Ann. I've spent a lot of time thinking over the last week. Do you know anything about me and Adrian, other than what you saw at your dinner party.'

I lie and say no…nothing at all.

'It all began at your wedding…I set my sights on him from the first moment I saw him. There was just something about him that set my vulva on fire…'

Again, too much information;

'After your wedding we saw so much of each other Ann. The sex was mind blowing…but it wasn't just that, we had a connection.'

This is all starting to sound a bit familiar…has Adrian not just said almost exactly the same thing?

'I think I love him, Ann. Can you believe it? Me, Sylvia the infamous flamingo who has just wanted no strings sex all these years has finally fallen in love. Sadly it can never be…I'm twice his age. His Mother was disgusted and I'm sure his mates would take the piss…it wouldn't be fair to put him through that and let's face it as soon as someone younger with perkier breasts comes along he'll be off. I haven't spoken to him since that night…it's probably fairer for us both that way.

Fucking hell….they love each other. He doesn't care about her age, but she thinks she's too old for him…it's like a Shakespearean tragedy;

'Maybe Sylvia, you need to let Adrian make that decision. Maybe he loves you too? How will you know unless you speak to him.'

'I don't want to take the risk Ann. I've been on my own for so very long…I'm scared to fall in love. I don't want to get hurt again. I've also got to consider Josh…what would he think if he knew my new boyfriend was just a couple of years older than him.'

I think Josh would be fucking delighted to see Sylvia with someone…better that she concentrates on her own love life than interferes in his. She sits herself down and starts to sob quietly. This is all too sad. Hearing Sylvia cry is obviously too much for Adrian and he hurtles down the stairs. She looks shocked to see him and just as she's about to tear a strip off me he begins to speak;

'Don't blame Ann, Sylvia. I've been upstairs listening to everything you've been saying. I love you Sylvia…you move me like no woman ever has done before and the things you do in that flamingo mask. I don't care how old you are. I don't care what anyone thinks…I want to be with you and just you. We really could have a future together. My Mum will come round eventually and I'm sure me and Josh could be mates. Let's give it a try Sylvia…we won't know unless we try.'

Sylvia stops sobbing and I don't know which way this is going to go. Slowly she goes into her handbag and pulls out the flamingo mask…she puts it on, gets up and literally jumps into Adrian's arms;

'I love you too Adrian and I do want to try, I really do! Ann, would you mind if we pop upstairs for five minutes?'

Erm, yes Sylvia I do fucking mind!

'As much as I love you Sylvia and as fond of my cousin as I am…no, there is no way you can go upstairs for a quick shag…take him back to your house, for God's sake.'

As they leave, Adrian turns and kisses me on the cheek;

'Thanks Cuz. I owe you one.'

'You owe me nothing, now fuck off and stop calling me cuz.'

Sylvia and Adrian are now officially a couple and I made it happen…I feel like Cilla Black. I really don't know how Aunty Maureen is going to react but if she wants to keep her son she's going to have to be a little bit more accepting. I make out tea and wait for Archie to get home…I have so much to tell him. I put the telly on and settle down to watch Coronation Street when there is another knock on the door. How did I get so popular? I look out of the window…it's Archie's Mum! Before I can duck down and hide under the window sill she sees me and waves. Bollocks, I'll have to answer the door now…what could she possibly want with me? I let her in and she actually seems quite pleasant…she clearly doesn't have a stick up her arse today;

'Ann, I wanted to come and apologise to you. I haven't been particularly pleasant since you married Archie. Archie has been the apple of my eye since he was a little boy. Don't get me wrong. I love his brother just as much, but there was always something a bit special about Archie. As he grew up I convinced myself that no one would ever be good enough for him. He had a few relationships before he met you but they never lasted long. When he told me he was getting married, I thought I'd lost him and I resented you for that. I can see you're good for Archie…you are strong and stand your ground. You certainly didn't let me walk all over you. I want to welcome you into our family with open arms…you are the Mother of my grandchild and you clearly make my son very, very happy. Can we start again? I promise I'll never mention the names Phyliss and Edgar again.'

What could I say? Of course we could start again...I wanted everyone to be happy. By the time Archie came home me and his Mum were chatting like we'd been friends for years. I've never seen him look so surprised as when he walked into the kitchen and saw us sharing a packet of chocolate digestives. She told me all about Archie as a baby and I was horrified to learn that when he was born he weighed in at a mammoth 10 pounds and 8 ounces...that's not far off 11 pounds! If this baby takes after it's Father I won't need to worry about pushing in labour...it's going to walk out. So all in all it's been a strange but successful day. Sylvia and Adrian are sorted and I've been invited into the bosom of Archie's family...what more could I ask for?

CHAPTER SEVEN

Boy or girl?

I can't believe I've hit 20 weeks of pregnancy already…time is flying by. I'm half way there and I'll have gorgeous baby in my arms in no time. If you had told me a couple of years ago that I would soon meet the man of my dreams, marry him and have his baby I would have thought you were fucking deluded…I really did snatch victory from the jaws of defeat. I definitely have a bump now…it's not huge but I am most certainly, noticeably pregnant. Not long to go now before I'll be in those much craved maternity knickers. I'm delighted that my sickness has completely gone…I can finally walk into a café again without heaving at the smell of crispy bacon. I feel strangely energised and I'm pleased to report my sex drive has returned with a vengeance. Just as I was starting to think I would never feel like a shag again, it just crept up on me one evening when we were watching telly. Archie put his hand on my knee and my muff suddenly sprang back to life…it wanted it's fill of Dr Gorgeous and nothing was going to stand in it's way. It took us a little while to figure out how we were going to do it…me on top, sideways, doggy style? It turns out all of those alternatives were fucking fantastic. Check me out…Ann without and 'e,' pregnant erotic goddess and rocking the reverse cowgirl. Things have been much better with Archie's Mum since we had out chat. We are actually getting on really well. It did cross my mind that she was just grooming me in order to get me to agree to a Phyliss or an Edgar but I really do think she's genuinely grown to like me. Today is going to be such an exciting day. We have our 20 week scan today and we have decided we want to know the sex of the baby. I've never been one for surprises and at least we'll be able plan ahead if we know what we are having. 'Planning ahead' how very grown up and organised of me…it must be down to the pregnancy hormones.

I'm waiting for Archie outside the maternity unit…my bladder is full and I'm beyond excited. He arrives and we make our way to the waiting room. Once we get there I tentatively pop my head around the door just to check there's no surprises of the Miss Fucking Perfection Personified variety waiting for us. Thankfully it's all clear…I don't need to worry about her fluttering her eyelashes at Archie today. After a short wait we are called in for our scan. It's the same routine as last time with the very glamorous paper towel tucked into my knickers and a liberal amount of cold gel smeared on my ever expanding belly. The sonographer turns the screen towards us and begins the scan…and there it is, our beautiful little squidge. I can't believe how much bigger the baby looks…it's pretty obvious it's going to look bigger but it doesn't stop you marvelling at it. The room is silent as the sonographer takes all the necessary measurements. We just watch in awe as our baby wriggles about and I swear it just waved at me. Once she's finished the sonographer confirms that baby is healthy, growing and doing all the right things;

'Would you like to know the sex of baby?'

Of course I wanted to know the sex of the baby. I really wanted to know;

'No thank you. I think it would be nice to have a surprise.'

What the fuck just came out of my mouth. Archie looks confused but not half as confused as I am. What the hell happened to being organised and planning ahead? I really, really wanted to know but just for a split second I thought it might be nice to wait and see. I had to fucking vocalise that one random thought didn't I? Before I could say I'd changed my mind the scan had finished and our photograph had been printed off;

'I thought we were going to find out the sex Ann, how come you changed your mind?'

'I don't know Archie…I just opened my mouth and the word 'surprise' popped out. Are you terribly disappointed we didn't get to know.'

'Of course I'm not…it's going to be the best surprise in the world. You go to the loo. I just need to make a quick phone call before we head home.

He's such a sweetie and he's right, it is going to be the best surprise ever. There's a queue for the loo so it's a few minutes before I join Archie at the car. He's still wandering about with his phone. It looks like he's trying the same number over and over again or trying multiple numbers and getting nowhere;

'Who are you trying to call Archie?

He looks really sheepish…that's not a good sign;

'Just the dry cleaners to see if they can fit my suit in for a clean next week.'

He's also a really shit liar…who the fuck calls their dry cleaners? In the car on the way home I start imagining the worst. Who was he calling? Could it be another woman? Was it Miss Fucking Perfection Personified? I look at today's scan picture and my eyes start to well up. Could he really betray our baby for tits and teeth? As we pull into our driveway my head feels like it going to explode. I get out of the car as quickly as my bump will allow and march to our front door and flinging it open I let Archie have it with both barrels;

'Are you fucking Miss Perfection Personified?'

He doesn't respond but our families and friends do;

'SURPRISE!!'

What the actual fuck is going on? As I walk through the door I'm showered with pink and blue confetti. Oh shit! Archie gently whispers in my ear;

'I was trying to get hold of Sylvia to tell her to call the surprise gender reveal party off…and how many times do I have to tell you…it's you and only you.'

So what was I supposed to do now? Tell them we haven't got a clue if we're having a boy or a girl or wing it and take a guess. There was a 50% chance we'd get it right. They had gone to so much trouble. There were pink and blue balloons everywhere, they'd had an amazing pink and blue bootee cake made and the buffet must have cost a fortune. I make an excuse about needing Archie to get something out of the car for me and drag him outside;

'Archie…what the fuck are we going to do? They've worked so hard to make it special for us.'

'Firstly Ann. I only want you…always and forever. Please stop comparing yourself to that awful woman. She could be the last woman on earth and I wouldn't be interested. As for the party, we could tell them the truth or we could toss a coin…heads for a girl, tails for a boy?

Ultrasound scans are never 100% accurate so if we get it wrong we just pretend to be surprised when the baby is born. What do you think?'

'I think that's a brilliant idea…go on toss the coin.'

Archie flips a ten pence piece into the air. He catches it and flips it onto his hand…tails, we're having a boy!

We go back into the house and start to mingle with our guests. Luckily they didn't hear my little outburst as I opened the door, they were far to busy trying to shout surprise in unison. Apart that is from my friend Veronica who could hear a pin drop a mile away;

'Ann, you daft twat. You've got to stop obsessing over that Camilla woman…I know she copped off with Daniel and stole Ryan from you but that's in the past. Archie isn't going anywhere. He's clearly devoted to you and you have to accept that and stop being so insecure.'

She's completely right and I have been letting my Camilla paranoia get the better of me. I'm not going to give her another thought. Our guests our passing round our scan picture to a chorus of oohs and aahs. As for me, I'm heading straight for the buffet table…I've got weeks of not being able to eat properly to make up for. As I'm sitting quietly in a corner stuffing myself with mushroom vol-au-vents, Sylvia and Adrian come into the kitchen. They obviously haven't seen me as they start full on snogging next to the kitchen sink. I suddenly start to feel a bit queasy…which is nothing to do with my pregnancy and everything to do with cousin Adrian playing tonsil tennis with Sylvia less than a metre away from me. I try coughing but they don't register me at all…it's all getting a bit heated so I walk over and tap Adrian on the shoulder;

'Oh sorry Cuz, we didn't see you there. Shit, I forgot you don't like me calling you Cuz do you? So when are we going to find out about this sprog then.'

Of course he forgot not to call me Cuz. Since we were children he's made it his life's mission to wind me up. In fairness I have given him plenty of ammunition over the years and although he irritates the shit out of me, he's making Sylvia happy so he can't be all bad. I tell Sylvia I'm ready to do the reveal and she gathers everyone in the lounge. She's given me and Archie a confetti cannon each…Archie has the blue and I have the pink. She counts down from five and whichever one of us has the corresponding cannon to the baby's sex has to fire it into the air. Archie fires his cannon and our guests are covered in blue confetti…'It's a boy' shout mine and Archie's Mums in unison. I do feel a bit bad about lying to everyone but I would have felt worse if all this had gone to waste. The room is full of excited chatter about boy's names and blue pram blankets. I make a point of telling my Mum not to go overboard on the blue…we want to dress our baby in all the colours of the rainbow.

It's been a lovely evening but I'm relieved when everyone leaves to go home. I'm absolutely knackered and just want to relax with my Dr Gorgeous. It takes us ages to clear up all the confetti…it's one of those ideas that's great, when you don't have to do the cleaning up afterwards. I snuggle into Archie and suddenly feel what I think is wind in my stomach. It happens again but this time it's stronger. Suddenly it hits me…it's Baby Gorgeous and can feel it kicking!

'Archie, quick give me your hand. I can feel the baby kicking.'

Archie places his hand gently on my stomach and we wait. I feel another little kick and Archie nearly jumps off the settee with joy;

'I felt it Ann, I felt our baby kicking.'

We both stare at my tummy in awe and wonder…it won't be too long before we meet you little one. It was the perfect end to a perfect day…just me, Archie and Baby Gorgeous.

CHAPTER EIGHT

35 Weeks and Counting

Where has the time gone? It feels like yesterday that I first did my positive pregnancy test and now here I am entering the last few weeks of my pregnancy. I've really bloomed since my 20 week scan…I'm fucking huge and occasionally wonder whether they missed a twin. I haven't seen my feet in ages let alone my poor abandoned muff. I really should give it a courtesy trim before I go into hospital but as I can't see it, my bush will just have to grow free. It wouldn't surprise me if Bear Grylls turns up when I'm in labour to help the midwife negotiate my untamed fanny jungle. Sadly, after a few blissful weeks of fanny tingles, my sex drive has plummeted again. I'm too tired and feel too heavy for any jiggery pokery…I can just about summon up the energy to give Archie the occasional sympathy wank. As for my appetite for food…I can't get enough of it! I have two specific cravings. The first always comes in the morning. I have to have to have a bacon butty followed by a packet of chocolate mini eggs. My second craving can come on anytime and multiple times a day…beef Monster Munch washed down with a mint hot chocolate. It's that beefy, minty combination. I can't get enough of it. Consequently I've put on three stone…three fucking stone! Even my much desired maternity pants are starting to feel a bit tight. I've reached a point where I literally have to roll myself off the sofa as there's no way I can get up on my own. According to the midwife baby's head is now engaged, hence my open legged waddle, constipation and constant urge to pee…pregnancy is so glamorous! Baby is still very active…mostly when I'm trying to sleep. I can't tell you how strange it is when you can see various body parts poking out from my bump. A foot here and an elbow there…it really does feel like they are trying to break out and run free. I've made a mental note not to watch the film Alien until after they are born.

I've just popped into town to get fitted for a nursing bra and then later we've got an antenatal class…the last one before baby is born. I feel like the dog's bollocks as I walk into the posh lingerie shop. I'm convinced my pregnancy breasts are huge…you can't put on three stone and not get a whopping pair of bosoms. I stick my chest out and walk over to the shop assistant with a definite 'look at my huge titties' air about me. Once in a changing room the lingerie specialist takes the appropriate measurements…'36C' No, that can't be right. I was a 36C before I was pregnant…granted, I did have to pad the cups out a bit but come on. I ask to be measured again…I demand a recount! I stick my chest out even further in the hope it might give me an extra cup size. But no, I'm still a 36C. Well that's a bit of a disappointment. I put my top back on and as I leave the changing room I glance back and catch a look at my bottom in the changing room mirror. That's when it hits me. I have put three stone on my arse…a stone and a half on each butt cheek. Oh well, if I look on the bright side…I could now set up an Instagram account devoted to my shapely butt. I leave the shop with four nursing bras and my pride slightly dented. I immediately know what will make me feel better and head to the nearest café to order a bacon butty and I was very pleased to find there was a newsagent next door so I could pop in there to get my chocolate mini eggs. I manage to wait until I get home before I devour the butty and eggs in quick succession…they were so good! Baby Gorgeous is kicking away and judging by the way they are headbutting my bladder I think they enjoyed my lunchtime feast as well.

After a quiet day eating, reading and checking my hospital bag for the hundredth time I'm off to meet Archie for our antenatal class. He's running late when I arrive at the hospital and when he finally gets to me, the class has already started. Everyone is seated when we enter the room and as I quickly look around for free seats a familiar figure waves and beckons us over;

'Archie…come and sit here with me and Ryan.'

Miss Fucking Perfection Personified…I should have fucking known I wouldn't be able to escape her. They haven't been at any of the other classes we've been to, so why the fuck are they here today? Why did she only mention Archie, can she not bring herself to say my name? Archie starts to walk towards them and I pull on his shirt;

'They're the only available seats Ann and there's no way you can stand up for the next hour.'

He's right of course and I'd look a bit of a twat if I sat on the floor. I make sure it's me that takes a seat next to Camilla...she looked furious when she realised I'd foiled her plan to get Archie to sit next to her. Ryan nods his head and mouths 'hello'. He looks even more downtrodden than he did the last time I saw him. I'm guessing that when their baby arrives, it won't be Camilla doing the night feeds. The midwife runs through everything we have learnt from the previous classes from induction to emergency deliveries, from birth plans to feeding. I'm not really listening to be honest. I'm distracted by just how perfect Camilla looks even when heavily pregnant. She has the neatest of baby bumps and doesn't look like she's put on so much as a pound in weight. Camilla looks like a pregnant super model...me, I look like a fucking Moomin. My birth plan is sorted...drugs, drugs and more drugs. I'm not bothered about hypnobirthing or a water birth...just give me something strong enough to get rid of the pain and I'll be happy. The one thing I do want is an active birth where I can move around freely without being stuck on a bed. Apparently gravity can speed up labour and that's got to be a bonus. Eventually the midwife asks if anyone has any questions and the questions asked are pretty standard…what do I do when my waters break? How long until will I stay in hospital for? That is until Camilla opens her mouth;

'Can I wear make up when I'm in labour?'

Typical Miss Fucking Perfection Personified! The midwife has a little chuckle as she answers;

'Feel free to wear make up when you are in labour. You might find it gets a bit smudged as you go along though.'

'That's absolutely fine. Ryan will touch it up between contractions for me…won't you Ryan?'

Ryan shuffles uncomfortably on his chair and doesn't answer. He really didn't know what he had let himself in for when he started dating her did he?

The class ends and we mill around for a bit and chat with some of the other parents to be. Camilla spots we haven't left yet and strides purposefully over to Archie with Ryan carrying her handbag and following reluctantly in her wake;

'Hi Archie. Why don't you and I'm sorry, I've forgotten her name join us for a drink in the café?'

Of course she's forgotten my fucking name…that woman is absolutely shameless. Well I'm not taking any more of this bullshit;

'We're a bit busy this evening…maybe we could do it another time or maybe never? Ryan…what the fuck are you doing carrying her handbag. Is she so precious she can't carry her own bag?

Ryan looks uncomfortable as he hides Camilla's handbag behind his back. We've started to attract a bit of an audience as Camilla walks right up to me. We are literally bump to bump as she sneers in my face;

'I'm sorry Angela…I wasn't talking to you. I was talking to Archie and what my Ry, Ry does or doesn't do is none of your business. You're old news darling, he didn't want you and soon Archie won't want you either.'

There's a collective gasp from the small crowd that has formed around us. I can't believe I'm in the middle of an antenatal class having a Mexican bump off with Camilla. How dare she even suggest Archie will leave me and fucking Angela...who does she think she is? Who is this woman that is stalking my life? What did I ever do to make her hate me so much...is she a long lost sibling out for revenge because my parents abandoned her? Was she one of the 'cool' girls from school and I don't recognise her? Whatever her motivation, if I didn't have high blood pressure before I think I've got it now. Archie can tell by the colour of my face that I'm about to explode and expertly diffuses the situation;

'My wife is right Camilla, we are busy this evening and just so you don't forget for next time, her name is Ann.'

What does he mean 'next time?' I'm not planning on seeing that woman ever again. I smile smugly, slip my arm through Archie's and we head out. Can you believe it...she's actually trying to pull my husband not only in front of me but in front of her own partner. The woman has no shame. I can't help myself, as we are leaving I turn round and give Miss Fucking Perfection Personified the middle finger. A couple of the other Mum's clap at my act of defiance. Her face is an absolute picture and Ryan belly laughs until she gives him the scariest death stare I think I have ever seen. Having won that round I'm hoping that's the last we'll see of Ryan and Camilla. I'm seriously thinking of calling the hospital when I go into labour to check they are not there…I would quite happily have a home birth with no pain relief whatsoever if it meant I didn't have to see that dreadful woman.

I think I must rant about Camilla all the way home and only start to calm down when we pull into our drive. I think I need to call in an exorcist because that woman is haunting me. Archie helps me waddle into the house and just as I settle down to a packet of beef Monster Munch I feel a twinge. It's nothing major and I don't mention anything to Archie as I most likely have wind. The last thing I want to do is present at the hospital only to deliver a huge fart. But after about half an hour I seem to be getting pains every few minutes;

'Archie…I think I'm having contractions.'

Archie leaps out of his seat, runs upstairs to get my hospital bag and grabs his car keys. He's actually panicking…Archie a doctor who has spent years training for situations just like this one, is actually panicking…I start to feel slightly superior;

'I don't think the hospital is necessary yet Archie. I've only been having them for about 30 minutes.'

He's clearly beyond excited but agrees we need to time the contractions and get a better idea of what's going on. Archie watches me like hawk and notes down the time of each contraction…he's back into doctor mode now which is a lot more reassuring than the running around like a headless chicken mode he was in when we got home. Over the next couple of hours the contractions start to get quite close together and just as we think 'this is it' and make the decision to call the maternity unit…they stop. I'm assuming they must have been Braxton Hicks contractions which are something I'll have to get used to over the next few weeks. Baby Gorgeous will come when he or she is ready and if they are anything like me, that moment will be when we least expect it.

CHAPTER NINE

Hello Baby Gorgeous

The past three weeks have passed really, really slowly. I'm now 38 weeks pregnant and if I thought it wouldn't be possible for me to get any bigger I was wrong. My bump has grown so much I'm convinced I'm going to give birth to a toddler. I had to get Archie to cut my toenails the other day and although tempted, I stopped short of asking him to give my muff a good trim. I'm not sleeping very well as Baby Gorgeous is still partying the minute I try and sleep…it's good practise for their teenage years I suppose but as a consequence I haven't got the energy to do anything more than sit in front of the telly covered in Monster Munch crumbs. I've got so many stretch marks my backside looks like aliens are trying to send us a message…not so much crop circles as arse circles. Our respective Mother's have been very attentive. I have a freezer full of casseroles and my Mum hasn't stopped knitting since we told her I was pregnant.

They call me pretty much constantly wanting to know how I am or if anything is happening yet? No matter how many times I tell them I will phone them the minute I go into labour they just keep on calling. It's really sweet of them but I didn't answer the other day and my Mum rushed round with a first aid kit...she'd got it into her head I was giving birth in the bathroom and couldn't get to my phone. What she thought she was going to do a packet of plasters, two wipes and a small bandage I don't know?

I'm waiting for Sylvia to come round...she pops in most days on her way to work. I really look forward to seeing her as it provides a bit of light relief from the tedium of waiting. Suddenly I get a burst of energy and the urge to clear out my kitchen cupboards. I empty virtually every cupboard in the kitchen and when Sylvia arrives and lets herself in I'm standing on a chair scrubbing away;

'Ann, what the fuck are you doing?'

'Cleaning Sylvia...cleaning.'

I've become a bit frantic by this point. I've nearly got through a whole bottle of Zoflora and the kitchen stinks of 'Linen Fresh'…Mrs Hinch would be so proud.

'Ann, get down of the chair right now…a bump that size is going affect your balance.'

What the fuck is she trying to say? She helps me down from the chair…I didn't consider once I got up there how I was going to get down and makes a pot of tea. I feel calmer as a I sit at the kitchen table. Sylvia puts everything back in the cupboards for me and we settle down to tea and chocolate biscuits;

'I don't think you'll be long now…you've started nesting.'

Nesting…I've read about that. It's an Old Wives Tale apparently…I would have thought Sylvia would have known better considering she's a doctor. What next…baby will come this week because it's a full moon? As I'm laughing to myself I suddenly feel a sharp twinge in my stomach followed by what I can only describe as a pinging sensation. I leap up and look down as what feels like a tsunami of water gushes from between my legs.

Sylvia jumps up from her chair…I'm not sure if it's to help or to avoid getting soaked?

'Ann, your waters have broken!'

No shit Sherlock…of course my waters have fucking broken. As I'm surveying the puddle between my legs the pain starts…it feels like period pain only more intense;

'I think I need to go to hospital Sylvia…it fucking hurts!'

Sylvia calls Archie as I clean myself up and grab my hospital bag. I sit on a towel in Sylvia's car…it's fairly new and I think it's only polite to protect her upholstery from the vast amount of amniotic fluid I seem to be losing. Once I'm comfortable she jumps into the driver's seat and immediately puts her foot down…she's clearly watched too much Line of Duty because she's driving like she's on her way to crack a major crime syndicate. All we are missing is some 'chase' music and the scene would be well and truly set. I'm gripping the seat as she takes corners on what feels like two wheels. Fuck me, she's just jumped a red light…please don't let the police stop us. I don't want to give birth in the car. It's possibly the most terrifying five minutes of my life but at least it's taken my mind off the pain. Archie is waiting as Sylvia screeches to a halt outside the maternity unit...I have never been so relieved to see him.

We book in at reception and are shown into a delivery room and I put on my nightie and wait for the midwife. When she arrives she asks me to pop onto the bed and take my knickers off. I don't know if I'm confused because of all the pain but I immediately think 'why the fuck do I have to take my knickers off?' Oh yes, that's why...the baby is going to come out of my vagina. I was definitely a bit slow on the uptake there! The midwife waits for my contraction to pass and then has what feels like a good rummage around my innards. Apparently I'm really quite far along and baby won't be long at all...well that's a blessing I suppose. Archie helps me off the bed and I start walking up and down the room...I was determined to walk this baby out;

'Can I have drugs now then please. I'll take whatever you've got on offer...I'm not fussy.'

After listening to baby's heart beat she goes off to get me gas and air. I'm so far along she'd rather I just try with that for now…fucking marvellous. Once the gas and air arrives, I fling that mask on my face and breathe in for all I'm worth. I must admit it's quite nice…it gives me that couple of glasses of Prosecco feeling. As the midwife leaves she suggests I try the birthing ball in the corner of the room…I look at her in fucking disbelief as Archie brings it over to me;

'Come on, Ann, give it a try. It's really useful for helping open up your pelvis. Do you remember you tried it at one of the classes.'

I'm in pain, he's talking to me like a child and to add insult to injury. He wants me to bounce around on a fucking glorified Space Hopper?

'No thanks Archie…it was bouncing around on your balls that got me into this position in the first place. I think I'll give it a miss if you don't mind.'

I know he was only trying to help but I just wanted him to leave me alone…I wanted to get on with it and get this baby out. After about an hour, I've really had enough of him fussing round me. I love him dearly but he's been as much use a chocolate teapot…and when he actually started bouncing around on the birthing ball I'd had enough. I tell him…well order him to go and get a coffee but he's reluctant to leave me. After a bit of persuasion and admittedly a couple of threats he leaves me…but only for five minutes. As I puff on the gas and air I think back to how I ended up here…what a rollercoaster ride I'd had. Who'd have thought when I first met Archie in A&E we'd end up married and back in the same hospital still talking about my vagina.   True to his word, he is away no more than five minutes. Our Mums send their love and he had to persuade them not to come to the hospital…well that would be all I need. Why don't we invite everyone and have a party in the fucking delivery room….arrgggghhhhh!   Archie rushes over to hold my hand…I swear if he tries to mop my brow again I'm going to punch him. He tries to encourage me to breathe through my contractions like we learnt the antenatal class. I really am trying to remember to do my breathing but it's all starting to get a bit intense now.

Having seen numerous births during his years in medicine Archie recognises things are moving really quickly and presses the bell for the midwife.   I'm standing by the bed, legs akimbo and clutching onto the gas and air like my life depended on it. As the midwife gets on her knees to have a look, my fanny feels like it's on fire…

'I can see babies head.'

That explains it then…the infamous 'ring of fire' and never have I heard a more accurate description. My poor fanny does indeed feel like it's about to burst into flames. I try and listen to the midwife's instructions. Push, don't push…oh make your fucking mind up! Eventually babies head is out and I can hear Archie and the midwife having a conversation with it…'hello' 'hello little one.' Fucking 'hello' it's not even out yet and right now gravity is making me feel like I'm not only going to give birth to a baby but all the rest of my internal organs as well. After what feels like an age I give one more push and a beautiful, loud, crying baby appears from between my legs. The midwife places the baby in my arms and in that instant all the pain is forgotten. Archie cuts the cord and babe in arms, I'm helped back onto the bed. The midwife settles the baby on my chest and we are so smitten by its beauty we completely forget to even check what we've got. We have a quick look and…it's a boy! What a stroke of luck. We made the right call at the gender reveal party…we've got a little boy. Archie kisses me tenderly on the forehead;

'I'm so proud of you Ann and I couldn't love you and my son more.'

The daft twat is going to make me cry. The midwife takes the baby off to weigh him and check everything is as it should be…he weighs 8 pounds and is strong and healthy. He latches onto my breast and after taking an album full of photos Archie phones the family. His Mum cries, my Mum cries and after flying into the delivery room to get a first look at our son, Sylvia cries;

'He's beautiful you two…I assume I'm going to be his Godmother?'

Archie looks slightly horrified, but I couldn't think of anyone better;

'You are top of the list Sylvia…but you have to promise me you won't teach him any bad habits.'

'Not even burping the alphabet?'

'Especially not burping the alphabet!'

After Sylvia leaves, it's just me, Archie and our son. Our beautiful Jude…or as Archie keeps reminding me our beautiful Jude Edgar. He has a mop of thick black hair and he looks so much like Archie. I have never felt joy like this before and the love I have for my son is overwhelming.

CHAPTER TEN

Lessons Learnt

Baby Jude is one month old today. It's been an interesting month. Motherhood is certainly an interesting learning curve…babies don't sleep very much do they? Jude is just like me…constantly hungry and when I'm not feeding him, I'm changing his nappy. How can something that small poo so much? He loves having a bath and I'm sure he smiled today…although all my books say it's wind I'm convinced it was a real smile. I was singing to him and my singing is enough to make anyone laugh. Archie has been utterly brilliant, he's taken to being a Dad like a duck to water. So much so, he thinks we should have another baby as soon as possible…dream on Archie, dream on. The Nanas are absolutely smitten with him. As I thought, Archie's Mum thinks he's Archie's double in every way and she insists on calling him Jude Edgar. It's a bit of mouthful so I'm hoping the novelty soon wears off. My Mum can't keep away. She's here every day for a cuddle and if that means I can have a quick bath or a nap I'm not complaining. Even cousin Adrian has paid us a visit. Granted it was with Sylvia and he was more interested in playing with Jude's toys…but he still came. Who would have thought that in the space of a just over a year I would have got engaged, married and had a baby…so what exactly have I learnt from the experience, where do I start?

The first lesson learnt was when your partner gets down on one knee and proposes accept gracefully. Don't grab the ring like you life depends on it because when that sparkly fucker flies out of the box, there's no guarantee you'll get it back. Next, weddings are an absolute nightmare to organise. Everyone wants to have a say. From your dress, to the venue, to your bridesmaids…every one seems to have an opinion but the only opinion that is important is your own. It's your day, no one else's so do what makes you happy. You don't have to impress random relatives you've never met…bigger is not necessarily better. You're getting married because you love your partner and that should be the main focus of the day. Always, always get a copy of the best man's speech before the reception. Archie's brother Simon is the sweetest, quietest man and I would never in a million years have expected him to make my minge mishaps a major part of his speech. Thankfully most of our guests were pissed and had a sense of humour but my Mum has flashbacks every time she watches the wedding video and I'm not sure I will ever be forgive for showing her up in front of Aunty Maureen. However baby Jude has brought me some much needed brownie points.

Another important lesson was learnt on our honeymoon. When you find yourself in the swimming pool fuelled by lust and driven by alcohol. Always remember to double check that the supposedly secret hidey hole you have discovered is actually secret before you have sex. Believe me it's a bit of a shocker to discover that the people you've had polite conversation with at breakfast for nearly two weeks have just watched you having a quick shag. To avoid all confusion I would suggest you take all activities of the sexy time variety out of the pool and back into your hotel room. I'm still half expecting we'll appear in a women's magazine;

'Cheeky honeymoon quickie caused my Grandma to have a heart attack.'

Grandma would be fine but they'd still all have sad faces in the article and I would forever feel responsible for the near demise of an OAP. I also learnt that it is possible and quite likely that you'll get pregnant as soon as you come off the pill. Especially if you are partial to random daytime sex in a swimming pool. My pregnancy was a complete surprise…but what an amazing one! Which leads me on to…it is almost impossible to keep a secret. We managed to keep my pregnancy to ourselves for such a long time but in the end Sylvia figured it out. I guess she's keeps so many of her own secrets she can spot one a mile off. So if you have a Sylvia in your life and a secret to keep, either tell them what's going on or avoid them until you are ready to spill the beans.

I also learnt there is somebody for everybody. I would never, ever in a million years put Sylvia and my cousin Adrian together. I knew something funny was going on at my wedding and then to catch them in my shed…poor Aunty Maureen. It's not something I ever thought I'd be talking about. But they are blissfully happy and very much in love. They are just so right for each other and I wouldn't be surprised if we have another wedding to go to in the not too distant future. Adrian has just moved into Sylvia's house...Josh gave his full blessing. I think he's not only pleased to see Sylvia happy but he's fully aware that if she's distracted with her own life she'll keep out of his. Even Aunty Maureen has come round to the idea...Sylvia is such a charmer and she may be nearly twice Adrian's age but she's a doctor and that means social standing in Aunty Maureen's eyes. Will Sylvia give up her countryside activities...I fucking hope so Adrian is well smitten. It's taken Sylvia a lifetime to fall in love again...age is no barrier to anything. She's found her soul mate in Adrian...I haven't got a fucking clue what she see in him but something obviously clicked.

Pregnancy can be quite hard...especially those early months when I felt constantly sick but it's so worth it. Like weddings, once you find out your pregnant everybody has something to say about it. Listen to their advice, nod like you're really listening but only do what you feel comfortable with. I most certainly did not feel comfortable with naming my child Phyllis or Edgar. Archie's Mum was pissed off but came round eventually…to both me and the names. The whole Phylissgate saga also taught me that in a Mother's eyes no one will ever be good enough for her son. I already think no one will be good enough for Jude and once he's old enough to start dating they are going to have to get past me first. He's going to live at home with me until he's at least forty and then maybe he can think about marriage. There's a little baby girl out there somewhere who is one day destined to have me as her Mother-in-Law…I fear I'm going to make Archie's Mum look like a pussy cat. I also learnt that sometimes it's best not to vocalise your thoughts…can you believe I turned down finding out Jude's sex at the scan because I randomly thought a surprise would be nice. Which of course led us to the surprise gender reveal party which wasn't because we had no gender to reveal. I had visions of giving birth, then calling the family and telling them the scan was wrong and would they mind changing the all the blue things they'd bought for pink. I can't believe we guessed right…I must have known deep in my heart that Jude was a little boy.

I was pissed off to learn that Miss Fucking Perfection Personified is still turning up where I least expect her to. For fuck's sake what were the chances of her being pregnant and having a scan at exactly the same time as me? Why do our lives seem to intertwine so much? I suppose I'll never know but I'll be happy if I never see her again. How dare she treat me like I didn't exist whilst trying to reel Archie in with her shiny white teeth and fabulous tits. I've finally learnt that none of this matters. Archie loves me because I'm me…warts and all. He's not impressed by what's on the outside, it's your heart that really matters. Camilla may be gorgeous on the outside but she's pretty rotten on the inside. I have to admit. I am really curious to know what she had…I bet it was a girl and the minute she popped out she would have had a big, sparkly bow placed on her head. Poor Ryan, imagine having two Camillas to deal with. I'm not giving Miss Fucking Perfection Personified another minute of my headspace. How could I even contemplate that Archie would try and contact her...I blame my hormones.

My arse learnt the hard way that eating copious amounts of bacon butties, chocolate mini eggs, Monster Munch and mint hot chocolate can make you put on quite a lot of weight...they are fucking lovely though! Strangely now Jude is here, I haven't once felt the urge for a bacon butty. Can't say the same about chocolate though. I can't get enough of it...well I have to keep my strength up for breast feeding don't I? I'm not even thinking about losing any weight...I've just had a baby and I am what I am. I'm learning to embrace my curvier body...it just grew a baby and I love it for that. As for labour itself...I learnt it fucking hurts! I went into a strange sort of auto pilot where I wasn't scared of the unknown. I just had the overwhelming desire to get it done. I didn't need Archie fussing over me...the amount of times he tried to put that fucking flannel on my forehead! I also learnt that the minute the baby is born you completely forget about all the pushing and the pain...it's like it never happened once you have your baby in your arms. Don't get me wrong...I remember it now and once my fanny starts tingling again, there's no way Archie is coming near me unless he's doubly condomed up. Jude may have given me cellulite, stretch marks and a bucket fanny but I love him more than life himself. It's been quite an adventure for me since I first embarked on my quest to become an erotic goddess. In Archie, I did truly find the perfect combination of Mr Romance and Mr Uninhibited. After some spectacular failures, I got there in the end and I would never have to worry about wax, whips and my hairy bits again...or would I?

If you haven't read the first book in the 'Wax and Whips' series ('Wax Whips and my Hairy Bits') here's the first few pages...

CHAPTER ONE

Me

I used to love reading romance novels, nothing modern, just good old fashioned Victorian romantic literature. It was a time of innocence, the pace of life was slower, the men more charming. A time where you didn't have to conform to female stereotypes online, where you never needed to ask 'does my arse look big in this' because everyone looked big in a bustle and no fucker was going to get a look at your arse until you had a ring on your finger. It gave me hope that there was a Mr Romance out there for us all and then suddenly it dawned on me that actually it was all a little bit dull. It took me a bit of time to realise where it was all going wrong, but then it became clear. These novels, lovely as they were, were missing one vital component…they didn't do cock.

My name is Ann, not regal Anne, just plain, boring, unexciting Ann. I often wonder how my life would have turned out if my parents had just given me that extra 'e'. I am thirty-two years old, no spring chicken and no stranger to the dating scene. I work in marketing which isn't as glamorous as it sounds and if I'm honest it bores the shit out of me. The search for my Mr Romance had led me to a succession of short, infuriating relationships where the sex had been no more exciting than a blow job and a quick shag (missionary position). I needed less Mr Romance and more Mr Uninhibited. I needed excitement, hot wax and a fucking good seeing to. I was single, more than ready to mingle and had read a shit load of Erotica so I knew exactly what I had to do in order to embark on a new sexual adventure. I wanted no strings sex, none of that emotional bollocks, just a good hard fuck and maybe a cup of coffee in the morning. I'm bored of feeling boring. I don't want to be Ann who's a good laugh, I want to be Ann who's amazing in bed, I want to be the shag that stays with you a lifetime, never bettered or forgotten.

My longest relationship had lasted nearly two years, Hayden. We met when we were both at university. I was so young and inexperienced I didn't really know what a good shag was. I lost my virginity to him after four bottles of Diamond White and maybe it was because I was pissed, or maybe because he was shit at shagging, but it was a completely underwhelming experience. There was no earth shaking orgasm, just the feeling something was missing and a sore fanny for a couple of days. We muddled along, foreplay was always the same, I gave him a blow job, he tried to find my clitoris…the man needed a fucking map. Sex was nearly always missionary, I'd sneak on top whenever I could, but he'd always flip me over for a quick finish. Maybe we just became too familiar with each other but when he started to not take his socks off when we had a shag I knew it was time to move on. He wasn't that arsed to be honest, I think he'd started to prefer his games console to me anyway and if he could have stuck his knob in it I'm sure he would have dumped me before I dumped him. My relationship history since Hayden has been unremarkable, hence my decision to ditch the romance novels and dive head long, or should that be muff long, into Erotica.

I'm suppose you could say I'm reasonably pretty and my face is holding up well, which is surprising given my twenty a day smoking habit, absolute love of kebabs and a probable dependency on Prosecco. My tits aren't too bad, they measure in at a 36C and I'm pleased to say they are still nice and perky and probably a few years off resembling a Spaniel's ears. My legs are long and shapely and the cellulite on my arse can be hidden with a good, supportive pair of knickers. Thongs just aren't going to happen, sorry Erotica but negotiating with a piece of cheese wire up my arse does not do it for me whatsoever. I've been researching my subject well recently, and one of the first rules when embarking on an erotic adventure seems to be that one must have a shaven haven, a freshly mown lawn, a smooth muff…I think you get the picture. I need to think carefully about how I am going to achieve my erotica ready fanny as the expression 'bearded clam' doesn't describe the half of it!

I don't fancy having my fanny flaps waxed and shaving isn't really an option as I'm petrified I'll get a shaving rash. So the only option I've got is hair remover cream. A quick trip to the shops and it's mission accomplished; my lady garden is smothered in intimate hair remover cream. It looks like a Mr Whippy with sprinkles but definitely no chocolate flake. It's not the most attractive look in the world, I'm staggering around like a saddle sore old cowboy, but it's going to be worth it...I am Ann without an 'e' and without pubes, a bald fannied paragon of sexual liberation. That bird with the posh name in 50 shades of whatever is going to have nothing on me! Though I have to admit, the undercarriage was a bit of a nightmare and to be honest it does sting a bit. At least I don't have to wait too long and then I will be smooth, shiny and....ouch...I'm fucking burning now! Burning is not right surely? Jesus, my flaps are on fire. Give me a minute I need to jump in the shower and get this shit off.

I just spent four fucking hours in A&E. I washed the cream off and my minge was glowing red and burning like a bastard which was almost bearable until the swelling started. I could feel my lips starting to throb, they were pulsating like a rare steak. I didn't want to look down, but I knew I had to…fuck me I had testicles, just call me Johnny Big Bollocks because that is what I had. I quickly checked Dr Google and the best thing for swelling is elevation and an ice pack, so I spent the best part of half an hour with my minge in the air and a packet of frozen peas clamped between my thighs. Needless to say it had no effect at all and it became painfully clear that I was going to have to haul my now damp, swollen crotch to the hospital. Never before have I felt so humiliated, having to describe in intimate detail my problem to little Miss Smug Bitch at reception;

'So, you've come to A&E today because your vagina is swollen'...

…well it's my vulva actually but let's not split pubic hairs, or try and get them off with cunting hair remover cream. Sour face huffed and puffed and eventually booked me in, I spent what felt like an eternity pacing around…I couldn't sit down, my testicles wouldn't allow it and by this time a ball bra wouldn't have gone amiss. The Doctor I saw, who was absolutely gorgeous (the one time I didn't want to show an attractive man my fanny) and, when he wasn't stifling a laugh, couldn't have been more sympathetic. I'd had an allergic reaction and he'd prescribe me some anti-histamines which would bring the swelling down, my labia would return to their normal size and other than some skin sensitivity for a few days I would be fine but under no circumstances was I to use hair remover cream again as next time the reaction could be even worse. Though what could be worse than the whopping set of bollocks I'd grown I don't know. So that's that, I'm going to have to go au natural. Which is fine by me, I'd rather have a hairy beaver than an angry one.

A few hours later and my muff has more or less returned to normal and other than feeling slightly itchy seems to be perfectly fine. I've crossed shaven haven off my to do list and need to carry on with my preparation. As you may have already gathered, I've got a lot of work to do. I've noticed in most of the Erotica I've read that the words penis and vagina are rarely used, so I need to practise my sexual vocabulary, I need to learn how to talk dirty…I need to do my Erotica homework. I've had another flick through some of my books and there's no way I can call my vagina 'my sex' I know strictly speaking it is, but for fuck's sake…'my sex craves you', 'my sex needs your sex' it's all sounds a bit contrived if you ask me so I think I'll check out the Urban Dictionary.

I've just spent a good hour trawling through and my God what an education that was. Either I'm more wet behind the ears than I thought I was or some of the things I've just read are made up, check out 'Angry Pirate'…that's not for real, is it? I'm ready to try some of the new words and phrases I've learnt. I need to be all pouty lipped and doe eyed as I look in the mirror, moisten my lips and purr:

'I want to suck your length'

'Do you want to drink out of my cream bucket'

'My clit is hard and ready to be licked'

'My vagina is the most magical place in the world, come inside'

What the fuck was I thinking, I can't say this shit! Firstly the doe eyed, pouty lip thing makes me look like I'm pissed and secondly I can't do this without laughing. I'm much more comfortable with 'do you fancy a pint of

Guinness and a quick shag'. I quickly give my head a wobble, comfortable is boring. I'm in this for the excitement and the clit tingling thrill (see I did learn something). Maybe I'll just opt for quiet and mysterious, let my body do the talking and my mouth do the sucking (I'm really starting to get this now). So that's the plan, my persona will be a sultry erotic goddess who doesn't say much, I'll be irresistible, a fabulous shag who doesn't want a conversation, no chat just sex.

The last part of my preparation is what on earth am I going to wear? If I'm going for the mysterious look does that mean I'm going to have to channel my inner sex goddess, or does it mean I go for a prim and proper, hair up, professional look? Maybe a combination of both, tight fitting dress, hair up and glasses, then I can do the whole taking my glasses off and flicking my hair down thing. The hair flicking thing however is a bit of an issue for me: my hair is naturally curly…really curly, at university my nickname was 'pube head' which probably tells you all you need to know, so I'm going to have to straighten it to within an inch of its life. From frump to fox…check me out. Today is going to be an exciting day.

I'm just waiting for the postman to arrive, I've ordered some proper lingerie. I've gone for two sets initially, traditional black and racy red. Shit, should I have ordered a dildo? I forgot about a fucking dildo and candles, I forgot candles! What about a butt plug…what actually is a butt plug? I can't be erotic if I'm not dripping hot wax on him whilst pleasuring myself with a multi speed vibrating dildo…okay, so maybe not at the same time but you get my drift. Handcuffs! Shit, I'm not very good at this, he'll just have to tie me up with my big knickers.

The postman came, and I swear he had a knowing glint in his eye when he asked me to sign for my delivery or maybe he just read the label on the back of the parcel, cheeky bastard. It took me a while to build up the courage but here I am, standing in front of a full length mirror wearing a bright red, lacy push up bra, matching arse covering comfortable pants, a suspender belt and black stockings. I'm not sure. My tits are standing to attention and look like boiled eggs in a frilly egg cup, they are virtually dangling from my ear lobes and I swear you can see my minge stubble. So the new plan will be to go for subdued or even better, no lighting at all. I think it's all starting to look really erotic... bushy fanny, no filthy talking and everything done in the dark. The scene is set and I'm ready to get out there. No strings, erotic sex here I come. Well, not quite, I need to sign up to a dating site.

I take a selfie of myself looking as sultry as possible (not doe eyed or pouty, we know that doesn't work) I decide to show a little bit of cleavage and a little bit of leg, but not too much I want to leave my potential dates gagging to see more...I'm such a temptress. I've written and rewritten my profile about twenty times, it has to be just right and I think on my twenty first attempt I've finally done it:

'Flirty thirty two year old,

I work in marketing,

I like to get my head down in both the boardroom and the bedroom,

I'm looking for no strings attached fun,

Hobbies include reading, cooking and amateur dramatics.'

I know, you don't have to tell me, it's painfully shit. Hopefully they'll just look at my profile picture and to be honest at this point I don't care, I've submitted everything and I am now a fully paid up member of a dating site.

It takes a couple of hours for my phone to eventually ping with a notification that I have a message, I'm trembling with excitement as I open it...

'You've got nice tits'

Fuck me, 'You've got nice tits' is that it? I mean it's nice he thinks I've got nice tits, but I was expecting a little bit more. No, hang on he's sent a picture...it's a dick! He's sent me a picture of his dick, eww I don't think I've ever seen such a stumpy little penis, it's got a hugely bulbous bellend which looks like it's going to explode at any minute and hang on, it looks like it's winking at me...I'm never going to be able to unsee that! I quickly delete the message, when my phone pings again...It's another dick, not the same dick, this one is long, thin and veiny as fuck. Maybe I'm being too fussy, knobs aren't supposed to be attractive are they?   My phone is quickly becoming a rogues gallery of ugly shlongs. I'm really starting to think maybe this wasn't a good idea, I know I said I wanted plenty of cock, but this wasn't exactly what I meant. Three cocks later and just as I am about to give up on the whole idea (maybe a pint of Guinness and a quick shag isn't too bad after all) I get a message from Daniel. I check out his profile and he actually looks quite fit, he's good looking, athletic and he didn't send me a dick pic....

What happens next?...buy the book to find out!

And...while I have you here I'd like to recommend another book of mine. The book is called 'Fakes, Freaks, Cheats, Liars and Celebrities' and it's an outrageous thriller set in the world of celebrity that is by turns very funny, shockingly outrageous and very, very dark...here's the book blurb and some sample chapters...

Fakes, Freaks, Cheats, Liars and Celebrities

Fame. Lies. Scandal. Drugs. Sex. *MURDER.*
Celebrities have secrets to die for.

Andrew Manning has spent 20 years saving celebrities from the consequences of their own bad behavior and is known in the business as' The King of Scandal'. But now some particularly difficult and demanding characters are about strain even his legendary abilities:

Shelley, model and fashion icon, who's determined not just to blackmail her equally famous husband but also to destroy him.

Joey, an insecure reality TV star, desperate to hang on to his celebrity, even if it means slowly poisoning himself to death.

The Producer, a king in the world of entertainment and a serial abuser of hopeful young wannabe's. But this time he's picked the wrong girl for his perverted pleasures. Charlie, morbidly obese, murderous mafiosi adviser to... Janey, pop music goddess, a celebrity with peculiarly sharp teeth and disturbing eating habits that are about to be revealed to the public by an ambitious young paparazzo.

And then there's Johnny, Andrew's partner, a psychopath with a heart of gold who's on a mission to murder as many celebrities as possible.

Will Andrew be able to reconcile the demands of so many different and desperate characters, and who's going to end up dead?

'Fakes, Freaks, Cheats, Liars and Celebrities' - four sample chapters

Please find to follow four sample chapters taken, more or less, from the beginning, middle and end of the book...

In this first extract we meet Janey, international superstar; mad, bad, dangerous to know and possibly a vampire...

JANEY. MAKING AN ENTRANCE

As the limo speeds away from Heathrow, Janey is delighted with the way things went. What an entrance! The moment she stepped into the arrivals lounge it had been total chaos: screaming fans, paparazzi, cameramen, microphones, journalists, police, security. All there for her, Janey Jax. She is a *star*. No one comes close to her. Rivals come, rivals go and still she stays at the top, numero uno. Untouchable. Look at that Missy Go Go. Where is she now? Nowhere. Skank.

Of course, she could have flown over in the private jet, but with a world tour about to kick off and a new album coming up she needed an entrance with maximum impact, at least that's what Charlie had advised and, as always, Charlie had been right.

The day's events have left her tired, though. So tired. People forget that she's not a young girl anymore. She may still look like she's in her twenties but, in reality, she's far removed from that happy decade. Nowadays, it takes hard work to keep looking as good as she does. Hard work and fresh, young flesh. Very young flesh. She hopes Charlie won't have any problems sourcing what she needs here in England. But, no, she shouldn't worry, Charlie is very capable. He knows what she wants, and he is bound to her. By blood. He is her creature.

In this second extract we meet foul-mouthed, homophobic Shelley. Shelley wants Andrew to blackmail her famous, gay husband into giving her a huge divorce settlement, but Shelley has her own dark secret…

SHELLEY. TIME FOR A QUICK SMOKE?

Finally, the slow and tedious drive through London's crawling traffic is over and Shelley arrives at Anthea's house in Holland Park, she always stays there when she's in London. She and Anthea are Best Friends Forever. They've known each other since way back, from when they were in "Girls Gone Wild." There were four girls in the (quite successful at the time) band but Shelley only ever really liked Anthea. Chardonnay and Alicia were bitches and cunts, and where they fuck are they now? Losers! They hadn't been smart, but Anthea and Shelley had been. Shelley had used the band as a base from which to start her solo career, Anthea had exploited her celebrity and good looks to grab herself an extremely ugly but ridiculously rich banker. Christ, Shelley can feel nothing but admiration for the way she played that prick! Led him by the fucking nose, married him, stuck with him for a couple of years, then divorced him, taking almost everything he had. Honestly, men can be such gullible dickheads, show them a bit of tit and a glimpse of snatch and, in no time at all, you can have them behaving like well-trained dogs!

Once inside Anthea's house (she has her own key, that's how BFF she and Anthea are), she makes straight for the beautiful living room and throws herself into a gorgeous sofa, dropping her Prada bag onto a gorgeous coffee table, which rests on a gorgeous carpet. Shelley *really* likes Anthea's place, she makes her mind up that she too will buy a home in Holland Park when the divorce money comes through from Jack faggotpants.

Yes, the divorce settlement, more money, more success…what a wonderful day it's been! It's going to be so great when Anthea gets back from her latest shopping trip. Shelley can't wait to tell her what's about to happen to Jack, how she's about to blackmail him into a *huge* pay out. Hah, she is *so* going to screw him! Nobody fucks with Shelley!

Shelley muses happily for some minutes about her upcoming freedom from Jack and her fabulous future career in America, until her thoughts stray, unstoppably, to that package, nestled comfortably in the Prada bag. She takes it out, rolls it around in her hands, a greedy and needing expression on her face. Using her sharp finger nails, she quickly tears at and then unwraps the cellophane from the package, to reveal a substantial, round rock of crack cocaine. She places the rock of crack on Anthea's gorgeous coffee table. Taking a nail file from her handbag she begins to chip away at the off-white coloured lump, which has a texture somewhere between wax and brittle plastic. Expertly she detaches smaller rocks from the main block, each new rock just the right size for a single good hit when smoked. There's loads of crack here, enough to last her and Anthea a couple of nights, if they don't go too mad! As well as BFFs, she and Anthea are also BDBs, Best Drug Buddies.

She loves her crack does Shelley, fantastic stuff. Okay, so maybe the next day you might feel a bit down, a bit paranoid, but nothing that can't be smoothed out with a few drinks. Or some more crack. And the hit, Christ the hit! Once felt never forgotten! She knows of course that she shouldn't really be smoking it, what with her being famous, rich and beautiful and in a responsible position due to her influence over the young people of the world, but the public just doesn't realise that being famous, rich and beautiful is very hard work. Every day is filled with questions. What should I wear? Am I slim enough? How's my make-up today? Have I got the right handbag for this or that occasion? Who should I be *seen* to be speaking to? Which party do I go to, and which should I snub? Where should I be this afternoon to stand the best chance of being papped? These are all difficult and complex questions. Being a celeb is a demanding business, not everybody can handle it. Her lifestyle involves a lot of a pressure, and the crack is Shelley's way of relaxing, of dealing with the stress she endures every day. She deserves it. She is e*ntitled* to it.

Of course she has been in trouble with the crack before, resulting in some fairly unpleasant media coverage, but she had dealt with that, although it did involve some help from that hideous queer, Andrew. But that's all in the past. She's much more careful now, more discreet, she'll never be caught again. "Never say never," says a little voice somewhere in the back of Shelley's head, but she chooses to ignore it.

Shelley wonders if she should smoke a quick rock before Anthea gets back? Why the hell not!

In this third extract we meet Joey, a handsome young reality TV star. Joey's career has gone into freefall after launching an expletive laden attack against the Queen of England on live TV. In an effort to save Joey's career, Andrew prescribes a convenient case of pretend 'celebrity cancer' but Joey has a plan of his own…

JOEY. "I LOVE THE VERY BONES OF YOU"

Joey is woken early that morning by the Philipina nurse, fussing around. Making sure all his wires and tubes are in the proper place, he presumes. Actually, is "woken" the right word? Does he really fall asleep and wake up nowadays, or does he just drift in and out of consciousness? Joey's not sure but he thinks probably the latter.

Yesterday was a big day for Joey, he's surprised that he got through it. Saying goodbye to his kids, Christ that was hard. He'd had pretty much a repeat conversation with his ma and da later on. He told them that he felt that he didn't have long left (a message that Joey knew Andy's dodgy doctor would reinforce to them). His mum kept saying "don't be silly, Joey lad, you'll get through this," but he could see from her eyes that she didn't believe it, and she could see from his that he didn't believe it either.

As he explained his (recently made up) philosophy of time as great circle, with spirits racing around it and meeting again and again as different people, but always instinctively recognising each other, well, he could see it seemed odd to his parents. At times they looked at him as though he was delirious, but he got over his central message to them. Then he explained that the twins would be their responsibility, that there was plenty of money coming their way after he died and, most of all, that he loved them dearly and he was grateful beyond words for everything they had ever done for him, that he was immensely proud that they were his parents. He wonders what they'd think should they ever find out the reason for his illness, not cancer, but his own self-administered poison. They must never know that. Joey is grateful that only Andy knows the full story behind his condition. His secrets are safe with Andy.

Having checked all his various tubes and wires, the nurse helps Joey, on his request, to move position in his bed, from lain flat to sitting up. Joey has very little strength and the poor girl has to push and pull mostly on her own. Joey's grateful that, though only a small woman, she seems to have surprising strength. Together, they get him into a sitting up in bed position. The nurse plumps up pillows behind his back, puts one behind his head. She asks him if he needs anything else, does he need the bedpan? No thanks (there's nothing in him to shit out), but could she open the curtains and maybe get him a small glass of water? Thank you.

The nurse opens the curtains, and daylight streams in. Joey thinks it must be a beautiful day outside. The realisation hits him like a physical blow. Shit. This is it. It's a beautiful day and it's this day that I'll leave this world. Today is the day I die. I'll not see any more beautiful days. I'll not see any more days, full stop. Joey is hit with a huge sense of loss. You know what, despite all the shit, all the grief and all the idiots and haters it really is a beautiful, beautiful world. His thoughts are interrupted as the nurse returns with his water. She holds the glass to his lips and helps him take a few small sips. He asks her to leave the glass by his bed.

Joey slips back into sleep/unconsciousness, he dreams. He dreams a gorgeous dream. If his dream were a film it would be in widescreen, Technicolor, 3D, high definition, the whole shooting match. He dreams he is with the twins, his ma and da are there, and Andy and three of his oldest friends from his Doncaster days: Liz, Helen and Susan. They're all at Blackpool Pleasure Beach. There's nobody else there, it's empty, fantastic, the whole thing open just for them! And Joey's body is well again, it's young, healthy, vital, it is whole.

In the dream everybody is having a great time, they eat candyfloss and donuts, the twins go mad in the arcades, piling a stream of coins, that just keep spewing from the machines like magic, into the slotties and video games. Then they hit the rides. There are no queues, nothing to pay, they just walk on. They do the Dodgems, laughing hysterically as they bump into each other, they enjoy twirling on the Teacups ride, whizzing through the air in the old Hiram Maxim flying machines, thrilled as they take a ride through time in the River Caves, pretend to get scared on the ghost train. Then after more donuts and candyfloss it's time for the grand finale: the Big Dipper.

They all squeeze close up together in one giant dream-sized Big Dipper car and they're off, racing along the track. Normally Joey hates this kind of thing, but this dream Big Dipper is special. It's fast but smooth and, surrounded by such happy friends and family, Joey feels totally safe and secure. The Dipper speeds along, slows as it whizzes round a sharp bend, and then begins to climb a hill that seems to go on forever. It soars high up above the Pleasure Beach, then up above Blackpool, and looking to his left and right Joey can see way beyond the town and far out to sea. All the other rides become small, toy town in size and now the hill is so high that the view is like that from a plane. Joey is aware that the Dipper is pushing up higher and higher into the sky and he looks down and beneath him he can see big, fluffy pink clouds, like the candyfloss he has just eaten. Then huge objects appear above Joey's head: vast, snowflake-like constructions made of sparkling, clear ice, desperately beautiful and delicate and filled with a brilliant and warming, white inner light and Joey knows that they are stars. He is amazed, fascinated. They are so beautiful that they move him almost to tears. Then, as if it had decided it could go no further up, the Big Dipper car begins to descend, travelling down a huge and straight slope that seems to go on and on and on. It charges down, faster and faster, the wind whistles through Joey's hair, he feels an exhilarating freedom, everyone is loving it, Joey is loving it. But then he feels himself detach from the car, sucked out by the wind caused by its downward plunge. He's not scared, though, not worried. This sudden detachment seems like the most natural thing in the world. He flaps his arms and, just he as knew would happen, he can fly. He flies after the Dipper car for a while, but he can't keep up with its breakneck speed and he sees his family and friends are waving back at him from the car and shouting. They are smiling, they are saying "goodbye, Joey, we love you." Joey calls after them "I love you too," and stops trying to follow. He knows where he must go now, and feeling light and happy he begins to fly upward, back up to those beautiful, snowflake shaped stars.

Suddenly, Joey's dream vanishes. He is awake, disturbed by some bizarre burning pain in his chest. He's pissed off, that was a lovely dream. If only he could have stayed there! The ever present nurse has seen him stirring and ask if he's alright, "I'm fine, love," he says but grimaces in pain, the nurse notices and asks if he would like morphine. He thinks about accepting, but this is his last day, he doesn't want to spend any more of it asleep or in that warm morphine haze, so he answers in the negative and asks the nurse if she has the time and she replies, "it's just gone three o'clock , sir"

"Please, don't call me "sir" anymore, it's Joey, and you, what's your name?"

"Amor, sir...Joey."

"Amor, that's a lovely name. Amor, I want to thank you for all the 'elp you've given me, you're a great nurse an' you 'ave a very sweet nature"

Amor beams from ear to ear and says "thank you, Joey, you're a kind man, a good man."

"Now then, enough of all this compliment swapping," says Joey trying to set a light tone, "'elp me sit back up will you?"

After some mutual huffing, puffing, pulling and pushing, Joey is back in a more upright position. Shit, he thinks,

Andy will be here anytime now. He checks the glass of water is still

by his bed. Yes, it is, good. So this it. The end. He has less than an hour to live. God! He's not scared though, that dream he had has been strangely reassuring. He's ready to go, happy to go, to be honest, glad to escape the pain and discomfit that's been the main feature of his life for so long now. Sorry to leave everyone, of course, but, following his new philosophy of life and death, hopeful that it won't be for ever. Joey is about as prepared to die as any man can be.

There's a quiet knock at his bedroom door. Slowly it opens and first one head pops round, then another and another. Amazing! It's just like his bloody dream! It's Liz, Helen and Sue. "My girls!" cries Joey in delight, "come in, come in, it's so good to see you!"

The girls move as one, they come to Joey in his bed, Liz sits one side, Helen and Sue sit on the other. They're all touches and greetings, kissing Joey's cheeks, holding his hands, running their hands through his once thick hair. "Your mam called us last night, Joey," says Sue, "she told us you'd love to see us and so here we are."

"You mean," says Joey "that she told you you'd best get down 'ere quick like, before I go."

"Well, she said you weren't good, but you're going to pull through this, Joey," says Liz.

"Liz, girls, its good of you to say that but truth is I'm dyin', but I'm ready, I don't want no tears or sympathy so you three pull ya selves together...anyway, tell me, you musta left Doncaster bloody early to get 'ere for now, how's things up there, then?"

And so it goes, Joey spends a delightful forty minutes chatting away to his three old friends. He's always loved these girls, they were his best friends at school (he never really got on with other boys, he can see now that that wasn't a failing on his part, he just pissed them off because he was too bloody good-looking). They remained friends after school, and when Joey became famous, they were always there for him, a shoulder to cry on when things were bad, a source of mostly good advice and someone to share his success with. They were never envious of that success, never asked for more than he could give, they were always true friends.

And then, sadly, this sweet little chat has to end, Andy has arrived. He's standing in the open door of Joey's bed room, looks very smart, thinks Joey. He likes Andy's suit, Armani he guesses. Joey waves Andy forward, saying, "Andy, come in, these are friends of mine from Doncaster, Liz, Helen and Sue, girls, this is Andy. 'e's a friend an' 'e kinda 'elps me out wi' me, er, legal stuff." Andy and the girls exchange handshakes and greetings, Joey can tell that Andy's a bit stressed and seems a bit hurried, he's moving a bit funny too, like somebody had kicked him in the balls. Joey senses Andy needs his attention so he says, "girls, Amor, can me an' Andy 'ave bit of privacy for a few minutes? There's some stuff I'ave to talk about wi' 'im, business, that sorta nonsense." Of course, nod the girls and the nurse and they make their way out of his room, Andy following and closing the door behind them.

"Joey," says Andy looking nervous, rubbing his hands together and smiling rather fixedly as he does so, "how are you and are you ready for this? Christ, sorry, that's a stupid question, I…I just don't really know what to say, I've never helped anyone top themselves before!"

"That's okay, Andy, it's fine, don't worry, I ain't never topped meself before so I don't know what to say either!"

"And you're sure that this is what you want, that this is what you really, really want?"

"Absolutely sure, I'm exhausted, I just can't fight to keep meself alive anymore…just one thing, though…it won't 'urt will it, Andy…?"

In this fourth extract we meet Carrie. Carrie works for Andrew but harbours her own secret desire for celebrity. We join Carrie after she's had a bruising encounter with the sexually abusive entertainment mogul, The Producer. Ashamed and angry with herself for being so naïve, Carrie wonders what on earth she should do…until she encounters an Angel in a coffee-shop who has some good advice for her…

CARRIE'S STORY

After running out of *that* man's office, Carrie fled deeper into the anonymity of Soho, seeking shelter and safety in aloneness. She sits now in one of those soulless chain coffee shops, on her own, seat by the window, hunched over a large mug of the brown, bland muck that passes for coffee in these places, steaming like a warm cup of piss on the table in front of her.

She is appalled with herself. She is jittery. She is shaking with shame and anger. How could she have been so utterly stupid as to have her own secret dreams of stardom when she works in the world of celebrity? She knows, better than most, that it is a world of fakes and freaks, trickery, lies, abusers and cheats. But no, despite that fact, despite the fact that she's got a great, well-paid, interesting job and has lovely workmates, despite all that she has her secret, stupid bloody dream of being a singer.

And because of that, she ends up in that office. With that man. That pig. Dirty, disgusting, pig. Invited in to "discuss her career." For goodness sake, how stupidly naïve. She should have known something was wrong when he started going on about how she was older than his usual type of girl, but so pretty and so fresh-faced and reached under his desk and pressed something that closed the door and blinds of his office. Then he started coming out with all that crap about trust and commitment and he asked her to take her top off. When she wouldn't do it the dirty old git became abusive, stood up, came up to her, put his face in hers, mouthing obscenities and stuck his hand between her legs.

That was her more than enough for Carrie. She kneed the scumbag in the balls. Hard. He fell to the floor, huffing and puffing in pain, and she aimed a quick kick to his face and was pleased to hear a satisfying crunch as his nose broke under the impact of her foot. From there she was right on her toes, round the back of the guy's desk, found the cheeky little button he'd pressed to lock the office door, pushed it, door opens, she jumps over the prostate figure of the revolting piece of filth and she's out of the office and out of the building.

Christ. What does she do now? She wants to punish the dirty, nasty pig: a knee in the balls and a busted nose isn't enough. She wants to screw him over, see him broken, destroyed, maybe even dead, not just for her but for all the other people that she is absolutely sure he's done this to before. But how? She knows the way fame and wealth work, knows there is no point going to the Old Bill or the media. Like that'll get her anywhere, this guy is far too rich and influential to be troubled by minor nonsense like police and press.

What on earth is she going to do? She needs to talk to someone about this, if not to get revenge then at least for her own sanity. Carrie pauses in her thoughts and stares down at her rapidly cooling mug of coffee-type drink. She looks up, and catches sight of an old tramp shuffling around the coffee bar, he's going from table to table, asking for money, getting nothing but refusals in the form of stunted shrugs and a half-mumbled "no, no." The tramp looks up from his latest unsuccessful prospect and his and Carrie's eyes meet. He is a ragged, dirty, rumpled man but, God, the eyes! To Carrie his eyes burn with an incredible intensity of intelligence and compassion. They are spellbinding. She can't understand why no one else has noticed them, why they should dismiss so readily a man who so obviously shines from his soul. The tramp smiles at Carrie, looking at her as though she's the exact person he's just popped into the coffee shop to meet. He heads straight for her table and in seconds, he is standing by her. He smells bad, of sweat and dirty clothes, but Carrie hardly notices, she is entranced by those eyes, waves of understanding and love seem to flow from them and she feels warm and comforted, as if someone has woven a net beneath her to catch her should she fall. She is convinced that she is in the company of an angel. A dirty, smelly, ragged angel, but an angel nevertheless. The tramp/angel opens his mouth and says to her to tell Johnny, Johnny will know what to do. Johnny will make everything right. And with that he turns away, walks out of the coffee bar and vanishes instantly into the crowds of Soho.

As if he had never been there.

Carrie is confused. She's calm and happy, her strange visitor has definitely improved her mood, but she's confused. Why did she think that the tramp was angel? After all, the idea of an angel disguised as a tramp walking through the streets of Soho is just silly…isn't it? But why did he know about Johnny? *How* did he know about Johnny? And why does she know as a matter of absolute certainty that she *is* going to tell Johnny exactly what that dirty, rich, famous, abusive piece of filth did to her?

'Fakes, Freaks, Cheats, Liars and Celebrities' is available now as an ebook and paperback.

Printed in Great Britain
by Amazon

43532296R00086